ONCE UPON A DREAM

MARY BALOGH
and
GRACE BURROWES

Published as a two-novella compilation, Once Upon A Dream, by Grace Burrowes Publishing, 21 Summit Avenue, Hagerstown, MD 21740.

Cover design by Wax Creative, Inc.

ISBN: 1941419267
ISBN-13: 978-1941419267

ACKNOWLEDGMENT

When we wrote our novellas, we did so without intending to harmonize the stories beyond setting both at summer house parties. When it came time to think up a title for the two-novella bundle, nothing memorable occurred to us. We turned to our readers for assistance, and Pat Elliot came up with "Once Upon a Dream." That struck us as lovely and appropriate to our novellas, so thank you, Pat Elliot, and thanks to all the readers who jumped in with suggestions.

Mary Balogh
Grace Burrowes

Another Dream

MARY BALOGH

CHAPTER 1

The sun was still shining down from a cloudless blue sky when one of the outriders rode up beside the carriage in which Eleanor Thompson was traveling and bent to rap on the window. Eleanor looked up from her book, startled, and removed her spectacles as the maid who traveled with her lowered the window.

"Storm's coming up fast behind us, ma'am," the man said, removing his hat. "Tom Coachman was hoping to outpace it, but he says it can't be done even if he springs the horses, which His Grace don't like his doing on account of it can lame them easy. We are betwixt and between posting houses and it makes more sense to press on than to turn back. Tom says we will stop at the first inn we come to. You will be quite safe, ma'am, till then. She looks like a nasty one, but Tom is the best. No one less than the best would do for the dook."

With which words of alarm and reassurance he pulled back to resume his place behind the carriage. Both he and the other outrider had been sent to Bath with the carriage and the coachman and footman and maid to convey Eleanor from the girls' school she owned and at which she taught to Lindsey Hall in Hampshire, country seat of the Duke of Bewcastle. Wulfric, the duke, was married to Eleanor's sister Christine. Traveling thus was undeniably luxurious though it always amused Eleanor to be treated like a grand lady.

She pressed her face to the window and looked back. Oh, dear, yes. Thick, dark clouds were boiling up from the west, and even as she watched a jagged streak of lightning sliced through them. A thunderstorm was frightening, even dangerous, when one was traveling. The rain alone could quickly turn the road to a muddy quagmire. Even as she sat back in her seat Eleanor noticed that the wind was getting up. It was bending the long grass in the meadow beside the road and slightly rocking the carriage. The thunder that succeeded the lightning was felt more than heard above the clopping of the horses' hooves and the rumble of the carriage wheels.

She had left Bath early this morning for what was usually an easy day's journey. She had looked forward to being at Lindsey Hall in time to take tea with Christine and Wulfric and her mother, who lived with them. It was possible too that Hazel, her other sister, would have arrived before her with Charles and their children. It was a rare treat for their whole family to be together, but this summer Lindsey Hall was going to be filled to the rafters with family and other guests for a two-week house party in celebration of Wulfric's fortieth birthday. It now seemed altogether possible that Eleanor would not get there today at all. She might be forced to spend a night on the road. She could only hope that at least it would be at an inn.

"Don't worry, Miss," the maid said. "Tom Coachman is the very best, like Andy just said."

Eleanor smiled at her. "We must hope, Alma," she said, "for the sake of the men out there with only the brims of their hats to hide beneath, that the next inn is not far off."

By the time they reached it, however, a squat, unremarkable building on the edge of an equally unremarkable village, the storm had caught up to them and was raging about them in the form of torrential rain and a wind like a hurricane and unrelenting lightning and thunder. Alma was reciting the Lord's Prayer with her lips though some of the words were audible—"...Thy will be done on earth...And forgive us our trespasses...But deliver us from evil, oh please, please, Lord..." Eleanor was gripping the leather strap above her head and the edge of the seat cushion on her other side and had her feet firmly braced on the floor as though by so doing she could stop the carriage from rocking dangerously in the wind and weaving and slipping over the muddy surface of the road. The carriage somehow made the turn into the half flooded inn yard and came to a stop without being blown over.

"Amen," Alma said aloud and Eleanor repeated silently.

A few minutes later they were standing inside a low-ceilinged taproom that smelled of stale ale and was probably dark and dingy even when the sun was shining outside. At the counter the innkeeper was dealing with a tall gentleman in a caped coat, who was bespeaking two rooms and a private parlor. Eleanor doubted the inn boasted such a luxury as a parlor, but apparently it did. There were also two bedchambers available. She hoped fervently there was a third. She did not imagine this place was often besieged by large numbers of travelers looking for lodging. Its main function was almost undoubtedly to provide ale to slake the villagers' thirst.

Eleanor thought the gentleman was portly until he half turned and she saw that he had a child snuggled inside his coat—a child with a mop of unruly blond hair. A girl of about nine or ten stood beside the gentleman. An older woman, dressed plainly in a black cloak with a white mob cap beneath her hood, probably the children's nurse, stood a little apart from them.

"You don't have to be afraid any longer, Robbie," the girl said. "We are safe in here, are we not, Papa? I was not afraid at all, was I?"

"You were very brave," the gentleman said as he signed the register and the child inside his coat peeped at the girl with one eye until he spotted Eleanor and covered the eye with his hand before ducking against his father again.

"There was nothing to be afraid of, was there, Papa?" the little girl asked. "Just a lot of flashes and cracks and mud. Is that not right, Papa?"

"It is always wise," the man thus addressed said, "to have a healthy respect for thunderstorms, Georgette. They can certainly do harm to man and beast, though not when one is safely indoors."

"And woman too, Papa?" the child asked.

"Assuredly," he said with admirable patience. "To woman too and girls and boys and puppies and pigs and slugs. Thank you," he added as the innkeeper handed him two large keys. "We will move out of the way now so that this lady can be served. I do beg your pardon for delaying you, ma'am."

He had turned to Eleanor and smiled, revealing himself to be a handsome as well as a patient gentleman. He had his hands full with the child, who had been scared witless by the storm, poor little mite, and the girl, who seemed the sort to ask a million questions even when all she was really asking for was reassurance. For who would not be frightened when caught out in such weather?

"That is quite all right," Eleanor assured him. "At least it is safe and dry in here." Though she had got more than half soaked just in the dash from the carriage to the door.

Tom Coachman, drenched and dripping onto the floor, dealt with all the business of engaging a room for her and quarters for the servants after the gentleman and his family had moved away. Tom was not wearing the ducal livery—that happened only when he was conveying the duke or the duchess—but there was an air of authority about him that commanded respect. Before many more minutes had passed, Eleanor was in possession of another of the large keys and was on her way upstairs with Alma while an elderly lady and gentleman took her place at the counter. There was, alas, no other private parlor for her use. She would have to eat her dinner in the small public dining room with other stranded travelers. There would doubtless be more. She was quite resigned to spending the night here, Even if the rain stopped at this very minute—and it showed no sign of abating—it was doubtful the road would be safe for travel before nightfall.

Her room was small and stuffy. It looked clean, though, and there were two beds, one for her and one for Alma. But, oh, the tedium of being delayed. The storm might have been kind enough to hold off for a few more hours.

"At least, Alma," she said, standing by the window and looking down through the rain at a water-logged stable yard, "the floor is steady beneath our feet."

* * * * *

The terror of the past hour had exhausted poor Alma. Eleanor persuaded her to lie down for a few minutes and then, when the girl was fast asleep and snoring, she went downstairs to see if there was a cup of tea to be had in the taproom or, preferably, in the dining room.

She was ushered into the latter by the innkeeper and was pleasantly surprised when he quickly brought to her table a good-sized teapot with milk, sugar, a cup and saucer, and a plate. He returned moments later, while she was still wondering about the plate, with a platter of cakes and pastries, all of which looked freshly baked and smelled altogether too appetizing.

"The wife is in her element, ma'am," he explained, jerking a thumb back in the direction of the kitchen. "As soon as we heard the first rumble of thunder a couple of hours or so ago, she says, 'Joe,' she says, 'we are going to get company before the afternoon is out, you mark my words,' she says, 'and that company will be Quality,' she says. And she fired up the range and the oven and set to work. I haven't seen her this happy since it snowed sudden last December and we squeezed eleven persons and two nippers in here for two days. You will have a dinner tonight that you will remember till next summer and beyond, ma'am, and no mistake. She used to be head cook up at the big house, did the wife, and mighty put out they was when she married me and up and left to come here."

"But how fortunate for travelers who find themselves stranded here," Eleanor said. "I expect you have a full house by now, do you?"

"Ten and two nippers," he told her. "Even the couple I thought I would be obliged to turn away on account of there being no rooms left ended up staying. They were willing to sleep on the benches in the taproom if there was nothing else available, but when I mentioned the old attic room that is half full of boxes and gets wet in one corner when it rains hard, they took it sight unseen. I did not charge them more than the cost of their dinner and breakfast, though. It would not have been Christian, would it?"

"You are very kind," Eleanor assured him.

No one else had come down for tea. She had the dining room to herself. It had been dark to start with but had grown perceptibly darker in the few minutes she had been here even though it was still only the middle of a July afternoon. Any hope that the storm had moved off for good dimmed with the light. It was about to return for an encore.

The tea was piping hot and on the strong side, as she liked it. She eyed the platter of cakes and pastries. She must eat at least one or the innkeeper's wife would be hurt. What a wonderful excuse to indulge her sweet tooth. She considered a piece of currant cake before taking a puff pastry oozing with thick cream instead. Only her waistline would know. It was a good thing high-waisted dresses were still in fashion. She jumped slightly at a sudden rumble of thunder followed almost immediately by the sound of a child's voice just behind her shoulder.

"I am delighted," the little girl she had encountered earlier said, "that we are not the only ones who have been forced off the road to be stranded here in what Papa declares to be the middle of nowhere. It would be dreary, I think, to have the inn all to ourselves, though even that would be better than being stuck in the mud somewhere out there. You are the lady who came in right behind us. May I sit on that empty chair across from you for a little while? It might be considered forward of me, I know, when we have not been introduced and I am only ten years old besides. But there is no one here to introduce us, is there, and no one who knows us both anyway. I am Georgette Benning."

She was a thin child with a narrow face, large brown eyes, and dark hair clipped back from her face and flowing in loose waves down her back. She was gazing solemnly at Eleanor, who really was not craving company, especially that of a talkative child. She spent her days with young persons, talkative and otherwise, at her school on Daniel Street in Bath. She had enjoyed her life there for several years after making the decision to teach rather than go with her mother to live at Lindsey Hall when Christine married Wulfric. She had enjoyed it so much, in fact, that when her friend, Claudia Martin, the former owner, married the Marquess of Attingsborough, Eleanor had taken over from her, purchasing the school with the aid of a loan from Wulfric, a loan he always tried to insist was a gift. Holidays were meant to be different from one's everyday life, however, and this was the summer holiday. There would be children at Lindsey Hall, it was true, but they would be someone else's responsibility. Eleanor had pictured herself spending several weeks of blissful peace and leisure, consorting with none but adults.

The child was starting to look anxious at her silence. A flash of lightning lit up the room, flickered for a moment, and then flashed even more brightly. Eleanor smiled.

"I am pleased to make your acquaintance, Georgette Benning," she said, "and would be delighted to have you join me. I am Eleanor Thompson. But will not your papa and your nurse be worried about your whereabouts?"

"Oh, no," the child said, seating herself opposite Eleanor as the thunder rumbled, crashed, and then rumbled again. "Papa is shut up in his own room, nursing his bad temper—or so he warned us when he closed his door, though there was a twinkle in his eye as there always is when he says such horrid things. What he really meant was that he wanted to escape Robbie's clinging and my questions. I do tend to ask a lot of them. It is my Affliction, according to Nurse, and she always makes it sound as though the word would be spelled with a capital A if it was written down. Robbie was terrified of the storm, which he thought was going to strike our coachman dead and us too inside the carriage, though he is always frightened of thunder and lightning anyway. He is tucked up in bed for an afternoon nap with Nurse to keep an eye on him, which she will need to do with the storm come back. She would not let me sit on the side of his bed because I was fidgeting. Ooh! That was a bright one, was it not?" Her eyes widened and she got half to her feet before sitting again. "Ooh! And a loud one."

"Indeed it was," Eleanor said as rain suddenly sheeted down outside and pelted the windows, the force of a driving wind behind it. "Perhaps you would like to take this chair next to mine."

"I am not at all frightened," Georgette assured her, getting to her feet once more and scurrying about the table anyway, "but I will. I shall not stay long. But I could not sit still upstairs, for the one book I pulled out of my trunk last night for reading today—I had finished the other one—is really very boring indeed though I have no one to blame but myself as I am the one who chose to bring it. It is *Robinson Crusoe*. Have you read it? There are almost no characters in it except Robinson, who is stuffy, and I always like lots of characters. Do you? And lots of adventure. Being marooned alone on an island is an adventure, I suppose, but it is a dull one, is it not? Nurse was looking reproachfully at me when I kept fidgeting on my own bed and turning pages to see if the story gets any more exciting though I could not see that it does, so I said I would go and sit with Papa for a while until Robbie fell asleep, but when I got outside the room I thought it would be mean to disturb his peace so soon and decided to come down here instead to explore and see if there was anyone down here who is not nursing a bad temper. It really is quite safe to come down, is it not? There are no highwaymen or desperate villains down here, only you. I don't think either Nurse or Papa will be very annoyed with me for coming, though I daresay they will both be cross with me for disturbing you. Do you find this delay very trying? Oooh!"

A very bright flash of lighting was accompanied by an almost simultaneous crash of thunder, and the child's hand closed tightly about Eleanor's arm.

"You must stay here for a little while," Eleanor said. "But as soon as the storm abates it will perhaps be better to return to your room before your father and your nurse realize you are missing and become alarmed. Will you have a cake or pastry? When the innkeeper appears, I shall have a glass of lemonade brought for you."

"Oh, I shall not bother," the child said. "Ooh!" She scraped her chair a little closer to Eleanor's. "They will be even crosser if they think I have invited myself to tea. Ooh! Here comes another one."

Eleanor set one arm about the child's thin shoulders as the thunder shook the inn. "It is tedious to find oneself held up in the middle of a journey," she said, "but at least we are safe here and not marooned alone and for an endless time as poor Robinson Crusoe was. There is something rather magnificent actually about a thunderstorm, provided one is safe indoors."

"Nurse says it is God being angry," the child said, "but I think that is silly, don't you? If God is just a crotchety old man, I do not see why we should have to sit very still on hard pews every Sunday at church worshiping him and being bored silly. Papa is thinking of sending me away to school. He says I am restless and inquisitive and school will do me good. He may be right. There would be teachers and lots of books, would there not, and other girls and plenty to do all the time, and I would find out about all sorts of things, perhaps everything, though I do not believe girls' schools teach Latin and Greek, do they? But I would not enjoy having to sit still and silent all day long and having to do as I am told without any chance to discuss any rules that seem silly to me. Mostly, though, I do not want to leave Robbie. He is five though he looks younger, and he is shy and timid and I don't think everyone should be trying to make him come out of his shell, as Nurse describes it, and behave like a proper boy and stop sucking his thumb, which he does not always do anyway, only when he feels the need for some extra comfort. Mama died when he was a baby and he misses her even though he never knew her. I did know her for five years though I cannot remember her as well as I wish. I look after Robbie, but I don't smother him, even though some people say I do. I let him be who he is, which Nurse says is wrong because he has to learn to be a man. Oooh! I thought that one was coming right through the roof."

She reached out for the creamiest pastry on the plate, twin to the one Eleanor had just eaten, and bit into it. Eleanor slid a napkin toward her.

"Your brother is fortunate to have you," she said. Poor little boy. What a tragedy to have lost his mother soon after his birth. And what a tragedy for this little girl, who was trying to take her mother's place and appeared to be too intelligent for her own good. She would need some very patient and understanding teachers if all that was good and bright in her was not to be stifled at school in the name of discipline and making a lady of her, indistinguishable from all her peers. Not all voluble children were intelligent, of course, but Eleanor would wager a great deal that this one was. The child's next question confirmed her in this belief.

"Do you think children ought to be allowed to be who they are?" she asked after sucking cream from her fingers. "Or ought they to be brought up and educated to fit in, to be what their parents expect of them and what other grown-ups expect of them? Is that what life is all about, Mrs. Thompson? Learning to fit in?"

Oh, dear. What a very profound question, and how difficult it was to answer. But Eleanor never brushed aside girls' questions, profound or silly. She tried always to give them due consideration.

"Allowing people to be who they are sounds like a very wonderful idea," she said. "But carried to an extreme, would it perhaps lead to anarchy? If wild children were permitted to become wild young persons and then wild adults, would society work? For we have to live in society whether we wish to or not. We have to share our world with other people. If we all did whatever we wished to do, we would almost inevitably clash with other people intent upon doing what *they* wished to do, and quarrels and fights and even wars would result as they all too often do anyway. On the other hand, mindless conformity is not a desirable thing either. The answer to your question ought to be a simple one, but it is not. I have lived a great deal longer than you, and I am still not at all sure how much freedom and how much conformity create the perfect balance in our lives. The answer lies, I suspect, somewhere between the two extremes. I have not answered you very satisfactorily, have I? And it is *Miss* Thompson."

She wondered if the child had understood a word of what she had said. But Georgette's eyes, fixed upon Eleanor, were alight with approval as she reached absently for a piece of fruit cake, broke off a corner, and put it into her mouth.

"No one else—*no one*—has ever even tried to answer me when I ask that question," she said after swallowing. "Everyone tells me not to be silly, that children are not real persons until they have been shaped into the people their birth and station in life have determined for them. Admittedly, I have not asked Papa, though. I shall think about your answer. I may decide that I do not agree, but I love that you have spoken to me as though I were twenty instead of ten going on eleven. Or as though I were thirty or forty. It is sometimes very tiresome to be a child, Miss Thompson. Can you remember that far back? Did you find it tiresome?"

"Having to go to bed when the evening was only half over?" Eleanor said, pulling a face.

"Having to eat the cabbage someone else has put on your plate when you hate and despise cabbage?" the child said.

"Having an adult remind you every single morning to wash behind your ears when there is nothing wrong with your memory?" Eleanor said.

"Having to be silent in company until you are spoken to," Georgette said, "even when you are bursting to say something?"

"Having to count aloud the number of brush strokes you give your hair each night?" Eleanor said.

"Being told which books you can read and which are beyond your understanding?" Georgette said.

They both dissolved into laughter.

"I do believe the worst of the storm has passed over," Eleanor said, turning her glance to the window as Georgette ate a jam tart, "though the rain is still coming down hard."

"Perhaps Robbie has fallen asleep by now," the child said. "I had better go up before you have to suggest it to me again. That would be lowering. Oh, dear, have I really been eating your cakes? I did not mean to. I was not thinking."

"I wanted only one myself," Eleanor assured her. "It would have been a pity for all the rest to go back to the kitchen. Apparently the innkeeper's wife baked them especially for all the travelers she guessed would be stranded here by the storm. I am very glad you joined me, Georgette. You have been interesting company."

"So have you," the child said. "But now I really must—"

"Georgette!" a pained and reproachful male voice said from behind Eleanor's shoulder, making her jump again. "Here you are, you wretched child, bothering a fellow guest, as I might have expected."

CHAPTER 2

Michael Benning, Earl of Staunton, sighed aloud as the second installment of the thunderstorm passed over and the rain lashing his window eased in intensity. He had given in to a selfish impulse and shut himself into his room for some peace and quiet. He had stretched out on his bed and set one forearm over his eyes while his valet pottered about quietly, cleaning off the splashes of mud his boots had acquired during the dash from the carriage to the inn and spreading his coat over a chair to dry. Michael had neither slept nor relaxed fully. It was not the storm that was to blame, however. It was his conscience.

Robert was abnormally fearful of storms among other things and had clung and whimpered throughout their ordeal in the carriage, refusing to be consoled or be passed to his nurse's arms. Had he fallen asleep in his bed in the next room despite the return of the storm? Was Georgette occupying herself quietly enough not to disturb her brother and not to drive the nurse to distraction? His daughter had uttered those ominous words—*this is stupid!*—a few hours ago in the carriage after closing her book and tossing it aside before gazing out at the scenery and commenting upon every cow and barn and church spire. She was the one who had first spotted the clouds moving up from the west.

It would have been more charitable to have taken at least one of his children himself. He could have cuddled Robert beside him on the bed here. Or he could have brought Georgette in here and played some word or card games with her or even taken her downstairs for some tea. A conscience was a damnable thing. Mrs. Harris was hired, after all, to look after the children. But no doubt she was as weary as any of them from the long journey—this was the third day—especially after the last hour of it.

He sat up and swung his long legs over the side of the bed, rested his elbows on his knees, and rubbed his hands over his face. He had better go and check on the children. Perhaps Robert was sleeping after all. Perhaps Georgette by some miracle was too. Perhaps even Mrs. Harris was. Dream on, he told himself as he pulled on his freshly polished boots and his valet helped him into a dry coat.

Robert was indeed asleep, curled up in a ball on his bed, one flushed cheek visible, his blond hair hopelessly tousled, the covers drawn up to his ears despite the stuffiness of the room. Of his daughter there was no sign.

"Georgette?" he whispered, his eyebrows raised.

"She went to sit with you," Mrs. Harris whispered back, looking suddenly alarmed.

"Did she indeed?" he said. "But she did not arrive. Why am I not surprised? One thing is certain, at least. She would not have ventured out of doors."

And it was not a large inn. She might be watching the cook prepare dinner and asking a million questions. She might be grilling any groom who was unfortunate enough to be indoors about his duties. She might be exploring the attics or the cellars and finding bats or mice or people to question. He went to find her.

She was down in the dining room, talking with a lone lady who was having her tea there—the same lady who had arrived at the inn just after them, if he was not mistaken.

"You have been interesting company," she was saying, demonstrating a great deal of kindness and forbearance since her words suggested that his daughter had been with her for some time.

"So have you," Georgette replied and caused her father to close his eyes for a moment, appalled by her presumption.

The rain sounded louder down here, perhaps because there were more windows.

"Georgette!" he said, approaching the table with long strides. "Here you are, you wretched child, bothering a fellow guest, as I might have expected."

She looked up at him, guilt written all over her face. The lady turned her head too. She had been wrapped inside a gray cloak when he saw her earlier, with the hood over her head. She was clad now in a stylish blue dress. Her fair hair was simply and neatly worn. She had a pleasing, good-humored face with fine, intelligent-looking gray eyes. Her hands, lightly clasped on the edge of the table, were slender and ringless. She was, he guessed, about his own age, which was forty. He remembered that she had a low, pleasant speaking voice.

"You must be Mr. Benning," she said. "I do apologize for keeping your daughter here and causing you worry. She has been kind enough to bear me company through the return of the storm. Being stranded unexpectedly is a tedious business, is it not, though it is to be hoped we are not doomed to be stranded as long as Robinson Crusoe was on his island."

That was the book Georgette had tossed aside earlier and declared to be stupid. She must have told the lady about it—and no doubt about everything else that occupied every last corner of her crowded mind.

"It is kind of you to be so gracious, ma'am," he said before turning his eyes back upon his daughter, who was smiling brightly in the hope, no doubt, of averting any wrath he might still be feeling. "You were fortunate, Georgette, not to be snatched by some villainous cutthroat and borne off across his horse's back, never to be heard from again."

"Oh, Papa," she said, "what villain would be out in this weather? I have been making the acquaintance of Miss Thompson, and I have been eating her cakes, though I did not intend to and did not even realize I was doing it until I noticed the sweetness in my mouth. I thought you would be cross if you discovered that I had invited myself to tea, whereas you would not be quite so annoyed at my merely holding a friendly conversation with a fellow guest who was alone and in need of company to keep her mind off the thunder."

She smiled even more brightly.

He set a hand on her shoulder. "You certainly will not want any more tea, then," he said. "Probably you will not even need any dinner this evening. Perhaps I will have it served just to Robert and Mrs. Harris and myself."

"You would not do that, Papa," she said, her tone wheedling. "I am sorry to have worried you, but Nurse was looking exasperated because Robbie was taking a while to go to sleep and I wanted to sit on his bed to soothe him but I was fidgeting instead, and then I was fidgeting on my own bed because I had nothing to do. I decided to go to your room, but then I remembered that you were nursing your bad temper, mainly on account of Robbie's having been terrified and my having asked you a stream of questions about thunder and lightning and why they do not usually happen together even though they are really the same thing. So I decided to be considerate and leave you alone and came down here instead."

It was appalling to think of what she was revealing to Miss Thompson—*you were nursing your bad temper.* Out of the mouths of babes…

"You have my thanks," he said dryly. "But now you may go back up to reassure Mrs. Harris, whom I left a few minutes ago in a state of alarm. Tiptoe and whisper, however. Robert is asleep."

She went.

"Miss Thompson," he said, "I do apologize, both for my intrusion and for your having had to put up with my daughter when I expect you were looking forward to a relaxed and quiet tea. She is…difficult. And precious," he hastened to add, though he could hear exasperation in his voice.

"Oh, very precious, I think," she said, her eyes twinkling at him and revealing rather attractive fine laugh lines at their outer corners. "And, yes, difficult, I can imagine, to the people who are responsible for her upbringing. I found her a delight."

"It is remarkably decent of you to say so," he said. "Had you been expecting to reach your destination today?"

""I had," she said, looking ruefully toward the windows. "It is not going to happen, however, and my hope is now fixed upon tomorrow. One day's delay is tedious. Another would be severely annoying."

"And a great deal more delay, as was the case for Robinson Crusoe," he said, "would be plain stupid—in my daughter's opinion, anyway."

She laughed. "I must confess," she said, "that it was never my favorite book."

"Or mine, though it is utter heresy to say so of an acknowledged classic." He laughed with her. "But I believe it was my saying so that persuaded Georgette to choose it as one of her traveling books."

"That is perfectly understandable," she said. "You are on a long journey?"

"We have been on the road for three days," he said. "This was to have been the last. But someone important—I cannot for the life of me remember who— once said that the only thing we can confidently expect of life is the unexpected. I have lived long enough to know that he was quite right. Or perhaps it was a she. It is foolish of us ever to expect that life will proceed according to our plans and expectations. Miss Thompson, I realize that I have bespoken the only private parlor this inn boasts. I suspect the dining room will be filled later. My children will be eating their dinner early. I would prefer to dine later especially if I can prevail upon you to join me. Perhaps it is impertinent of me to ask when we are strangers, but the circumstances are unusual."

She hesitated visibly. It was not at all the thing, of course, for a single lady to dine alone with a single gentleman. But the circumstances were indeed beyond the ordinary, and he could almost see her weighing that fact against the alternative, which was to dine alone in a small and potentially crowded dining room.

"After having tea with your daughter," she said at last, "I do believe I would find it quite flat to dine alone, Mr. Benning. Thank you. I will join you. At what time?"

"Eight o' clock?" he suggested. "The children will be ready for bed by then."

"Eight o' clock it will be," she said.

He bowed and returned upstairs. He must take Georgette to his room and do something with her for a while—play chess, perhaps. He had a traveling set in his bag, and she was getting good enough at it that he was beginning to enjoy their games. He had never simply allowed her to win. She would know and would scold him. But in the foreseeable future she might win without any help at all.

I found her a delight, Miss Thompson had said, and she had seemed to mean it. He had not come across many adults who shared her opinion, though a number of people were polite and pretended to be charmed by her. Miss Everly was one such person. She smiled whenever she encountered his daughter, and called her a sweet child—an inappropriate description if ever there was one. Through part of the London Season that had recently ended he had considered Miss Everly as a possible candidate for his second wife, though he had never taken the step of actually courting her. It was her mother who had suggested a boarding school for the child she always referred to as *dear Georgette*.

He opened the door of the children's room quietly. Robert was still asleep. Georgette was perched on the side of his bed, patting his back through the bedcovers. Michael was always touched by the tender devotion with which she treated the sibling who was as different from herself as it was possible to be. His guess was that she was trying to make up for the fact that Robert had no mother. Though she did not either, did she?

* * * * *

She would have quite an adventure to recount to her mother and sisters when she arrived at Lindsey Hall, Eleanor thought as she changed into her gray silk with the white lace collar and sat for Alma to brush out her hair and coil it into a more elegant knot than usual high at the back of her head. She would not after all arrive tomorrow all grumbles about the storm and the tedious night she had been forced to spend on the road. Instead she would make much of describing her tea with the large platter of dainties worthy of the finest pastry cook and Georgette Benning for company. And she would make a riveting story of her invitation to dine tête-à-tête with the child's handsome and charming papa in his private parlor.

She hesitated before reaching into her bag for the velvet box that held her brooch, which Alma proceeded to pin between the lapels of her collar. It was her one valuable piece of jewelry, a cluster of pearls given her by Christine and Wulfric for her birthday two years ago. She did have another precious piece, but only she ever saw the diamond betrothal ring she had worn on a chain about her neck ever since she had removed it from her finger after Gregory's death at the Battle of Talavera—oh, a long time ago when she was young and full of dreams of endless love and happily-ever-after.

She hoped the brooch was not too elaborate for the occasion, though the thought amused her. Even if she had rings and bracelets and earrings to match, she would still look the prim, middle-aged spinster schoolteacher she was. The invitation to dine was merely the courtesy of a gentleman who wished to repay her for entertaining his daughter this afternoon. Or perhaps he felt that dining with her really was preferable to dining alone or eating early with his children. Whatever the reason, she was thankful to him. The inn was indeed full and the dining room would be crowded. She would be self-conscious sitting alone at a table there. She had never before stayed on her own at an inn.

She sent Alma off to her own dinner in the kitchen and went downstairs, smiling inwardly at the flutter of nervousness she was feeling, as though she were on her way to keep a romantic tryst. Thank heaven no one could read her thoughts. The innkeeper was hovering at the bottom of the stairs, and it was obvious he had been waiting for her. He bowed, led the way to the private parlor, tapped on the door, and opened it.

"Miss Thompson, your lordship," he announced.

Your lordship? The gentleman was not simply Mr. Benning, then? He was not alone, either. The children were with him, Georgette all flushed and eager as she jumped to her feet, the little boy clearly alarmed as he scrambled up from his chair to press against her side and clutch one of her puffed sleeves, one eye hidden behind it. He did indeed look younger than his five years. He was a thin-faced, mop-haired, big-eyed child—the hair very blond, the eyes dark brown—and purely adorable. The remains of a meal were spread on the table.

"Oh," Eleanor said, "am I early?"

"You are not," the gentleman assured her, getting to his feet and making her an elegant bow. "We are late. Bedtime is never actually bedtime in our house or wherever we happen to be. It is always half an hour or so later. My children are experts at delaying the inevitable. True, Georgette?"

"But it was not me this time, Papa," she protested. "Robbie wanted to have a look at Miss Thompson. He had only the merest peep when we arrived here."

The little boy's second eye disappeared behind her sleeve as though to give the lie to her words, but it reappeared almost instantly and gazed unblinkingly upon Eleanor.

"My son and heir, Robert Benning," his father said. "Miss Thompson, Robert. Now would be a good time to make your bow."

The eye disappeared again and his father sighed.

"He is shy," Georgette explained. "There is nothing wrong with shyness, is there, Miss Thompson? If there were no quiet people in the world, there would be no one to listen to those who have not a shy bone in their bodies. Like me. It takes all sorts to make a world, do you not think?"

"I do indeed," Eleanor said. "I am very pleased to make your acquaintance, Robert, and I shall assume that in your mind you have bowed to me. Are we not fortunate that the storm is over and seems to have no intention of returning? We must hope for sunshine tomorrow morning to dry the roads."

The child peeped again.

"Nurse will be very cross with me if I do not send you up immediately or sooner," Mr. Benning said, addressing his children. "Say good night to Miss Thompson."

Georgette said it at some length, and the little boy spoke for the first time.

"Will you come up to kiss us, Papa?" he whispered.

"Wild horses would not stop me," his father said. "But it will be after I have dined with Miss Thompson, and by then you will both be fast asleep. In the meanwhile, I will kiss you now."

The little boy scurried over to him, clutched the outsides of his breeches, and raised his face, his lips puckered. Mr. Benning bent to cup his face and kiss him and then tousle his hair, which actually looked more like soft blond down than hair.

"Good night, son," he said.

"Good night, Papa," the child said. He darted a look at Eleanor before tucking his chin against his chest and muttering something that might have been *good night*.

"Good night, Robert," Eleanor said while Georgette was claiming her kiss from her father. "Good night, Georgette."

The little girl took her brother's hand as they left the room.

"I am sorry to have kept you waiting for your dinner," Mr. Benning said. "Please have a seat."

"Your lordship?" She raised her eyebrows as she sat and he moved to a small side table to pour them each a glass of wine.

"The Earl of Staunton," he explained, handing her a glass. "You need not *my lord* me, however. I am quite content to be Michael Benning."

Why was it, Eleanor wondered, that handsome men seemed to become even more good-looking as they aged while the opposite was true of women? He was solid of build with an elegant figure and dark hair beginning to recede at the temples but looking strangely attractive as it did so. His face, which had probably been purely gorgeous when he was twenty, now had the firmness of character and experience to make it all the more worth looking at. Or so it seemed to her. She had not known him when he was twenty. And she was not usually given to such analysis of a man's charms. She did not usually dine alone with single gentlemen either. The room seemed suddenly very quiet.

"To storms and the unexpected pleasures they sometimes bring," he said, seating himself and raising his glass.

"Indeed," she agreed, raising hers. Was he saying she was an unexpected pleasure brought by the storm? What a very nice compliment!

* * * * *

Georgette, her brother's hand still clasped in her own, paused at the top of the stairs before proceeding to the room where their nurse would be awaiting them. "Well?" she asked him in an urgent whisper. "What did you think?"

"You really believe she is the one, Georgie?" he asked.

"Oh, I do," she said with passionate conviction. "I really, really do, Robbie. Did you notice her eyes? They seem to smile all the time. And did you notice that she did not wait for you to make your bow to her? Instead, she agreed with me that it takes all sorts to make a world and said that funny thing about believing you had made your bow in your head. Then she went on to talk about sunshine tomorrow before Papa had a chance to insist that you bow *outside* your head as well as just in it. I really, really, *really* think she is the one."

"Our new mama," Robert whispered, his eyes wide and dreamy, as though he were testing the thought in his mind. "But does Papa know? And does she know? And what about Miss Everly?"

"If Papa marries Miss Everly," Georgette said, "I shall run away from home. I swear I will. I'll go to America and ride across it on a horse until I am so far away no one will find me. Ever. It's *huge*, America is, Robbie. If you were to put England down inside it somewhere and Scotland and Wales and Ireland too, no one would ever find *them* either."

"Will you take me with you, Georgie?" he asked wistfully. "And can Papa come too?"

"Not if he is married to Miss Everly," she said. "Though it would be horrid to go without him and never see him again, would it not? We will just have to see that it never happens. She does not like us any more than we like her. At least, she does not like me. And that mother of hers detests us both, even you, probably because you are the heir. Oh, Robbie, Miss Thompson is the one. I just know it. I feel it here." She smote the left side of her breast with one closed fist. "I think she likes us. Even me, though I talked her head off this afternoon and ate her cakes."

"But how is it ever going to happen?" he asked, more practical than his sister. "If the sun shines tomorrow, she will go on her way to wherever she is going and we will go on our way to where we are going, and we will never ever see her again. Even England is big, Georgie. I think."

"I will make a plan," she promised.

"But what?" he asked.

"I just will," she said. "I will think hard before I go to sleep. But do you agree with me, Robbie? For it is no good at all if only I want her. I might as well sleep instead of thinking if that is so. We both have to want her more than anyone or anything else in the whole world. Is she the one?"

"Yes," he said. "She is."

CHAPTER 3

Michael had been wondering if he had acted too impulsively in inviting Miss Thompson to dine with him. She was, after all, very clearly a gentlewoman of some refinement. Now, however, he was reassured. She had been kind to the children, and a smile still lurked in her eyes. He felt instantly comfortable with her and found himself wondering why when he had decided to look about him during the Season for a new wife, it was the young ladies upon whom he had turned his attention. He had not considered an older lady, someone closer to him in age and experience. It was not as if he needed more children, though some people might say it was his duty to produce a spare or two to go with his heir.

"You have delightful children, Lord Staunton," Miss Thompson said after the innkeeper and a maid had cleared the table and set it again for two.

"It is kind of you to say so," he said. "Georgette is too loud and Robert is too quiet. One would have thought the Creator in his wisdom might have balanced them out a little more evenly."

"Perhaps," she said, "the Creator in his wisdom knew exactly what he was doing."

Ah. He must remember that.

"Robert's extreme shyness was sweet when he was two," he said, "and endearing when he was three. It is worrisome now that he is almost six."

The innkeeper opened the door again, and his wife and the maid came past him, the former carrying a covered tureen of soup, the latter bearing a basket of bread. The older woman ladled out their soup, which had smelled so appetizing when the children ate earlier, and all three withdrew and shut the door behind them.

"It is altogether possible," Miss Thompson said as she picked up her spoon, "that your son's shyness would grow worse if he were forced to try to overcome it. He will probably always be quiet. It is unlikely, though, that he will always hide his face from strangers. He will no doubt find a way to balance his shyness with basic good breeding if he is allowed to develop at his own pace and learn to be comfortable in his world."

"His nurse, who loves him quite fiercely, I might add," he said, "sometimes sends him to bed if he refuses to greet a visitor. It is not a huge punishment, of course, for more often than not he simply falls asleep. But it *is* a punishment, nevertheless. It implies rejection, which she tells him can be avoided with just a little sociability and courteous behavior."

"And it is not for me to question either his nurse's method of bringing up her charges or yours," she said. "I do beg your pardon. There is no single right way of raising a child, is there, and those who have none of their own are invariably the very best parents in the world." Her eyes were twinkling.

"No, I beg *your* pardon," he said. "I did not invite you to dine in order to bore you to tears with my concerns over my children."

"Children are never boring," she said. "Oh, sometimes one would like nothing better than to run screaming from them and not stop for the next hundred miles or so, but it is never because of boredom."

"You have personal experience?" he asked.

"Only as an aunt as far as young children are concerned," she said, "and that is a remarkably easy task, for one can spend time with them when one wishes and walk away when one has had enough. One can ignore their mischief and whining and tantrums with the certain assurance that one is not responsible for dealing with them. I had a small taste of being solely in charge of a class of young ones, however, when I substituted a couple of times for my sister at the village school where she taught. Each time I was exhausted by the end of the day and quite feared I might never recover."

He laughed. "You were never tempted to be a teacher yourself, then?" he asked.

"Actually I was," she told him, "and gave in to temptation. But I teach older girls at a school in Bath—the youngest of them are eleven. I find the work both pleasant and rewarding, though at present, I must confess, I am in the process of escaping gleefully for a summer holiday of peace and quiet and sanity."

She needed to work for a living, then, though she was certainly a gentlewoman.

"And your very first day of peace and sanity brought you via a vicious thunderstorm into the company of my daughter," he said. "You must be wondering what you have done to deserve such punishment."

"Not at all," she said. "I know the answer. I lost my patience with one of my girls last term and needed the reproof. But what is one to do when a girl one has been shaping into a genteel young lady for two whole years shows her disapproval of another girl's actions by crossing her eyes, poking out her tongue, sticking her thumbs in her ears, and waggling her fingers—all after she has invited the other girl to shut her face? Such behavior would try the patience of a saint, and I have never come close to sainthood."

He laughed and relaxed further. He liked her.

"The thunderstorm was an annoyance," she continued, setting her spoon down in her empty bowl. "Your daughter was not, however. I hope—oh, I do hope, at the risk of interfering again, that you never think to deal with her by squashing her spirit. She needs a thoroughly stimulating education as well as many and varied and vigorous activities. And she does not need to be told that little girls are to be seen but not heard. There. Now I have become definitely obnoxious."

The door opened again and the innkeeper removed the empty dishes while his wife and the maid brought in the main course.

"Not obnoxious," he said when they were alone again. "I appreciate your comments. They reassure me. I am aware that I have a very precious child in keeping, but many people of my acquaintance would add a couple of letters to the description and call her precocious."

She smiled as she helped herself to vegetables. "She told me you were thinking of sending her to a boarding school," she said.

"Poor Miss Thompson," he said. "You cannot escape from your everyday life, can you? A lady of my acquaintance believes school would be good for Georgette, that it would t— Well, that it would tame her. Actually it was the lady's mother who made the suggestion, but Miss Everly agreed wholeheartedly with her, as she always does. Lady Connaught is a strong-willed woman."

Miss Everly was a sweet-tempered young lady as well as a very lovely one. Unfortunately she was also ruled by an overbearing mother.

"School may well be the very thing for your daughter," Miss Thompson said. "Or it may well not be. The school itself would need to be chosen with care, and her own wishes would need to be consulted even though she is only ten years old. In my school, no girl is accepted as a boarder unless she has given her free consent. School is not a jail but rather a portal to freedom, or at least it ought to be in an ideal world. It was my understanding this afternoon and my observation earlier this evening that Georgette is strongly attached to her brother. Do you see her as a bad influence on him? Do you perhaps blame his shyness upon her willingness to shield him and speak for him? Do you believe they need to be separated?"

He considered. And he could hear that very concern being expressed in the gentle, sweet voice of Miss Everly. She had said it in London a month or two ago the evening after he had taken her and his children to Gunter's for ices. He had feared that perhaps she was right.

"No." He frowned as he cut into his steak and kidney pudding. "No, I do not, Miss Thompson. Robert will be devastated if Georgette goes away for weeks at a time, and she will be devastated to leave him. But...is it the best thing anyway? Why does no one warn prospective parents of the momentous and torment-provoking decisions that lie ahead of them? But this is most definitely not your problem, and I do apologize again. Tell me about your family. You are going to see them tomorrow?"

"Yes," she said. "I lived in a village in Gloucestershire with my mother until a few years ago. Both my sisters married, one of them to the local vicar. She is still there. They have three children, two boys and a girl. My other sister returned home after she was widowed. That was when she taught part time at the village school. She was very good at it. The children adored her. Then she remarried and her new husband invited both my mother and me to live with them. My mother was keen to go. I was less so. Being a spinster of very moderate means suited me fine, but only provided it came with independence. Luxury and dependence in my brother-in-law's very lavish home did not appeal to me at all even though they were offered with graciousness and love. I might have remained alone at the cottage and eked out an even more frugal existence, but it would have upset my mother and my sisters and I do believe I might have been lonely. So I chose to teach—but older girls, whom I dearly love."

She was a woman of courage, then. How many ladies in her position would have chosen to teach when they might have lived in luxury with relatives who loved them?

"And you?" she asked. "Tell me about your family."

"My home is in Devonshire," he said, "not far from the northern coast. My father died suddenly when I was twenty-three, an event that put an abrupt end to my post-Oxford years of sowing wild oats. My mother remarried three years later and now lives in the north of England. I have no brothers or sisters, alas, but I do have aunts and uncles and cousins, almost all of whom live not very far from me. I married Annette when I was twenty-seven, and Georgette was born two years later, Robert almost five years after that. He looks like his mother, though she was not quite as blond or as curly-haired. There were complications after his birth. She never recovered her health and died six months later. I was fond of her. No, that is by far too bland. I was deeply attached to her and did not believe I would ever wish to replace her. It is only recently that I have come to two conclusions. One is that of course she cannot be replaced. It would be out of the question. However, that fact does not preclude my marrying again and having a quite different relationship with an entirely different woman."

"And the other conclusion?" she asked, setting her knife and fork side by side across her empty plate and picking up her wine glass.

"That perhaps it has been selfish of me to carry my mourning to the extreme of not providing my children with a new mother sooner," he said. "Georgette does not remember Annette very clearly, more is the pity, and Robert, of course, has no memory at all of her. I tell them stories about her and I hope I always will, but I do believe they have the need of a live woman to love and nurture them. I can give them a father's love, but I cannot be a mother too. I have tried and have felt my inadequacy."

"It must be difficult," she said, kindness softening her smile, "to choose someone who will suit both you and your children."

"Yes." He felt suddenly mortified to realize he was discussing his marital aspirations with a single lady whom he had invited to dine with him. An *attractive* single lady. "I do apologize yet again, Miss Thompson, for burdening you with my family concerns. You are altogether too good a listener."

"But I love listening to people," she said. "Really listening, I mean, to the words that people say and to what they do not say aloud. It is something I have learned at my school. Teachers tend to talk too much and understandably so because they have much knowledge to impart. But it is very important also to listen and to hear thoughts and emotions and the language of the body as well as spoken words."

She must be a very good teacher, he thought. Perhaps, if he decided to send Georgette to a boarding school... But he did not want to pursue that possibility any more tonight.

The innkeeper's wife and the maid brought in a steaming apple pudding and a jug of custard, and the innkeeper followed with coffee.

"I must commend you," Miss Thompson said, addressing the wife, "on the quality and abundance of the food, both this evening and at tea this afternoon. I do not believe I have ever been so well fed at an inn. Thank you."

The woman curtsied and flushed with obvious pleasure. "My only regret, ma'am," she said, "is that we don't get guests stopping here more often. I do love to cook and bake, I do." Her husband beamed at her with pride as they withdrew.

"You will be happy to see your family tomorrow," Michael said when they were alone again.

"I will," she agreed. "And we will all be there, Hazel and Charles and their children too. I have not seen any of them since Christmas and then it was for just a few days. This time I have been persuaded to stay for a whole month. Not that I needed a great deal of coaxing. Are you traveling toward Devonshire or away from it, Lord Staunton?"

"Away," he said. "But I am wondering if I have done the right thing. We spend the spring months in London because of my parliamentary duties, but I have always liked to remain at home during the summer, for the children's sake. I was persuaded to accept an invitation to a house party this summer, though, when I was assured that it is to include a large number of children of all ages. My own spend time with their cousins and a few neighbors at home, though not nearly as often as I would wish. They are alone together for days, even weeks at a time. It will be good for them to have others to play with all day every day for two weeks. But all the traveling is tedious, especially for them. May I offer you more wine?"

"No, thank you," she said. "I will have coffee instead."

They both relaxed back in their chairs, she with a cup of coffee in her hands, he with a fresh glass of wine, and talked upon other subjects—books, music, politics, London, Bath, and on and on. The conversation flowed effortlessly from one subject to another without any awkward pauses. Michael had not felt so relaxed and contented for a long while. Not in a woman's company, anyway.

He looked at her hands as they held and absently caressed her cup—slender hands with long, neatly manicured fingers. He looked at her dress, simply but expertly designed, and at the costly pearl brooch at her throat, her only adornment. He looked at her fair hair, prettily but not elaborately styled. And he looked into her smiling eyes with the laugh lines beginning to form at their outer corners and at her elegantly sculpted cheeks and rather wide mouth. At a mere glance he would not have considered her a beauty, and there was certainly nothing youthful about her appearance. He liked to look at her nevertheless. He guessed that she had never been extraordinarily pretty, but she had the sort of face and figure that had aged well and would probably continue to do so.

And why were such thoughts going through his head, interspersed with thoughts about the various topics of their conversation? Was it inevitable when one dined alone with a lady? How was she seeing him?

When she finally set down her empty cup and got to her feet, prompting him to do likewise, he felt regretful. Was the evening over so soon?

"It must be very late," she said. "There is no clock in here. And you have promised to look in on your children. I do hope neither of them is lying awake waiting for you."

"What a very pleasant evening it has been," he said, moving toward the door to open it for her. "I am actually glad we were both stranded here, Miss Thompson, though I was not at all glad when the storm forced me to stop at what looked like a sad apology for an inn."

"It has indeed been pleasant," she agreed, extending her right hand. "Thank you so much for inviting me to dine here with you. Good night, Lord Staunton."

"Good night, Miss Thompson," he said, taking her hand in his. But instead of shaking it, which seemed rather too formal a way to end the evening, and instead of raising it to his lips, as he might well have done, he covered it with his other hand and leaned across it to kiss her cheek.

She must have guessed his intent and turned her cheek to him. But while she was turning her head one way, he went the other and ended up kissing her on the lips. It could have—should have—been an extraordinarily embarrassing moment. If either of them had jerked away, it would have been. But neither of them did. He pressed his lips more firmly to hers, and she kissed him back while her fingers curled about one of his hands.

It was neither a long nor a lascivious kiss. He raised his head after a few moments, squeezed her hand, and released it.

"I do beg your pardon," they said simultaneously, and her cheeks grew rosy. They both smiled.

"I meant no disrespect," he told her. "I have enjoyed meeting you, Miss Thompson."

"And I you," she said as he turned to open the door. "Good night."

He was left feeling slightly hot under the cravat and a bit flustered and wondering if he owed her more of an apology than he had already expressed. But that would merely draw attention to what had surely been nothing of any great note.

He gave her time to return to her room before making his way up to his children's, where he dutifully kissed their sleeping cheeks and smiled at their nurse, who was sitting by the window in the light of a single candle, knitting. And suddenly he felt melancholy and very alone in the world despite these precious two children.

Perhaps the Creator in his wisdom knew exactly what he was doing, she had said. Perhaps she was right. Perhaps Georgette was perfect just as she was. Perhaps Robert was perfect just as *he* was. Indeed, he knew they both were. But ah, the responsibility of being a father, a single parent. He desperately wanted them to be happy. They desperately needed a mother.

It must be difficult to choose someone who will suit both you and your children, she had said. He closed his eyes briefly before leaving the room to return to his own. Yes, indeed it was. He must always think first of what was best for them, of course, but ah, sometimes it was difficult not to be selfish and long for someone to ease his loneliness, someone to love again.

And someone with whom he could relax in a late evening after the children were in bed, while they drank their wine and their coffee, and talk upon any subject under the sun. Someone to kiss and take to bed afterward.

Good God, *did* he owe her a more proper apology?

* * * * *

The sun was shining, the road was firm beneath the wheels of the carriage, the journey was drawing to its end, there was excitement in the expectation of seeing her family again soon, and...and Eleanor was feeling really rather depressed.

She knew why, of course. For she had almost made up her mind to have a talk with Wulfric, but it would take courage. He would be disappointed in her. He would consider her a failure. Her mother and Hazel and Christine would be disappointed too—and upset for her. But the truth was—oh, horror of horrors!—that she was not enjoying being owner and headmistress of Miss Thompson's School for Girls. She had had no idea when she took over from Claudia with such eager delight how different it would be from simply teaching. It was not just all the extra work, though that seemed endless and was wearying enough. It was more the distance the position somehow put between her and her teachers, much as she respected and even loved them all, and between her and her girls, whom she adored and for whose lives she was fully responsible. She longed to be just a teacher again, all the burden of everything else lifted from her shoulders.

She believed she had a prospective buyer. One of her best teachers had recently inherited a considerable and unexpected fortune from an aunt but had no wish to live upon it in idle luxury. She had made Eleanor an offer for the school and then laughed at her own absurdity when of course Eleanor had no thought of selling. Yet Eleanor suspected she had been more than half serious, and she had been sorely tempted to admit the truth there and then both to her friend and to herself. She had been sorely tempted ever since. But would it be an admission of defeat to step down? It was not that she had failed, though. Her school was thriving and it was a happy and productive place. It was just that *she* was not happy.

She stared sightlessly through the window and gave more thought to the lowness of her spirits. Was she being honest with herself about the cause? Could it be that she had fallen a little in love yesterday? With two young children and their handsome father? How very silly if it were true. The father was looking for a second wife and a new mother for the children, and he had mentioned a Miss Everly, whom he was surely courting if she and her mother were already making suggestions for his daughter's future. And even if he was not courting the lady, he would certainly not consider courting her. Not that she wanted him to do any such thing. Besides, she would very probably never see him again, and it was just as well if she was going to start behaving like the stereotypical old maid, getting all fluttery and simpery over an evening spent in company with a personable stranger. Ah…and over a kiss that had not really been a kiss at all. He had been intending to peck her on the cheek, as he might have done with a sister or a maiden aunt. It was just unfortunate that she had turned her head the wrong way and his lips had brushed her own instead.

Oh, more than brushed, Eleanor, she told herself. He had kissed her. And she had kissed him back. It was that second fact even more than the first that had sent her scurrying upstairs to her room and an almost sleepless night while she had relived the kiss over and over, just like a giddy girl.

Eleanor put on her spectacles and directed her eyes, though not, alas, her attention to her book. If it had been upside down, she thought with some disgust after a few minutes, she would probably not have noticed. But it was not. She read a whole sentence with concentrated attention and wondered if Georgette Benning was reading *Robinson Crusoe*.

At last the carriage turned between familiar towering gateposts and proceeded up the long, straight driveway lined with elm trees standing to attention like well-trained soldiers, until Lindsey Hall came into view. Eleanor closed her book and removed her spectacles. It was a magnificent mansion that melded so many different architectural styles as a result of addition upon addition being added through the centuries, all somehow blending into a glorious whole, that it would be impossible to describe it with a single label, like classical or Gothic or Elizabethan. It was all of those and more. The great fountain in the courtyard before the front doors, surrounded by a circular flower garden, was spouting water high into the air and creating rainbows of color with its spray.

The front doors stood open, and Wulfric and Christine, the Duke and Duchess of Bewcastle, were at the foot of the steps, Wulfric looking his usual austere self, Christine almost bouncing with excitement just like a girl though she was approaching her middle thirties. Hazel and her husband, the Reverend Charles Lofter, were coming down the steps with her mother.

Oh, it felt so very good to see them all. Anxiety and depression fled as Eleanor leaned forward and smiled.

"I would have laid a wager," Christine cried as Wulfric himself opened the carriage door, set down the steps, and reached up a hand to help Eleanor alight, "that you were held up by those dreadful storms yesterday, but alas, no one would bet against me. Wulfric declared that only a bad thunderstorm or an earthquake would prevail upon our servants to risk his wrath by stopping for a night on the road. Eleanor, how *good* it is to see you. And how wretched that we had to wait a whole day longer than we expected. Charles said it was a lesson in patience."

And then Eleanor was caught up in hugs and exclamations and kisses and laughter and all the women talking at once while the two men looked on and she wondered where they were now on the road—Georgette and Robert, that was. And their father. Michael Benning, Earl of Staunton.

CHAPTER 4

"Are we almost there, Papa?" Robert asked for the fourth or fifth time, a toy horse clutched in each hand, the game of racing them and jumping them over his legs having lost its appeal.

"Soon now," Michael said—as he had said four or five times before.

Mrs. Harris had nodded off, her mouth agape, her cap slightly askew. Georgette, arms folded, unnaturally quiet, was staring through the window beside her, sulking. She had wanted him to invite Miss Thompson to breakfast this morning but he had told her the lady must be left to start her day in peace. She had wanted to go and see if Miss Thompson was in the dining room, but there were other people in there and he had told her they must not be disturbed. She had wanted to find out which room was Miss Thompson's so that she could knock on the door to thank her for the tea and conversation yesterday. He had said no, that she had thanked the lady at the time. She had wanted to find out where Miss Thompson lived so that she could write a thank you letter in order to practice her penmanship—that last detail had been added hastily when she had suspected, quite rightly, that he was about to say no again. She had darted downstairs when they were leaving and peered into the deserted dining room before dashing to the counter in the taproom to ask the innkeeper about Miss Thompson's whereabouts.

"I just want to say goodbye, Papa," she had explained when she realized he had overheard.

But the lady had gone.

Perhaps, Michael thought now, he ought to have allowed her five minutes in which to say goodbye. She had been strangely taken with the lady, and Miss Thompson had seemed to like her too. Had he forbidden it only because he did not want his daughter to intrude upon her privacy? If he were honest with himself, must he not admit that he would have been embarrassed to see her himself this morning? That…kiss had grown in proportion during a night of disturbed sleep. It had certainly spoiled what would have been memories of a thoroughly pleasant evening spent with a personable companion.

Robert climbed onto his lap and yawned. Did all five-year-old boys seek such comfort from a parent? Or girls for that matter? It seemed to him that Georgette even as a toddler had squirmed and wanted to get down soon after either he or Annette had tried to cuddle her.

Perhaps he ought to have remained at home. But he had liked the Duchess of Bewcastle from the moment he first danced with her at a grand ball in London and she tore the broad flounce off the bottom of her gown with a loud ripping sound as her foot stepped on the hem. She had laughed with what was clearly genuine amusement, called herself a clumsy clod, gathered up the sagging flounce in one hand, revealing a shocking length of silk-stockinged leg as she did so, and made off for the ladies' withdrawing room as if such an embarrassment were a daily occurrence. When he had met her again at a private concert, she had invited him to her house party after discovering that he had two young children and rarely left home with them during the summer. Lindsey Hall would be positively teeming with children of all ages for two full weeks, she had told him, and they would all have enormous fun. He had accepted the invitation.

It had been such a long journey, though, and ended during an unexpected rain shower. The duke and duchess greeted them in the great medieval hall, and Georgette brightened somewhat at the sight of old banners and weapons displayed on the walls and an elaborately wrought wooden minstrel gallery at one end. Robert, as usual, had burrowed inside Michael's coat. He took them up to the nursery floor himself rather than pass them off to their nurse. The duchess accompanied them.

"The rain has driven the children all indoors," she said. "I believe it is just a shower, though, and not a return of yesterday's storms."

The large schoolroom on the nursery floor to which she led them did indeed teem with noisy, exuberant children, and Georgette brightened further. The duchess began to identify them.

"Though you will be deserving of some sort of medal if you remember," she said before she had got very far. "Even I have to stop and think sometimes. Perhaps I ought to have had name labels written for each of them and taped to their foreheads. There are my three and my sister's three and all of Wulfric's brothers' and sisters' offspring, who numbered fifteen at the last count, though Rachel—Lord Alleyne Bedwyn's wife—will be adding to that number before Christmas. And then there are the Marquess of Attingsborough's three though the eldest is not here at the moment. And there are the children of our other guests, including your two."

"At least," he said, "I will remember two names."

She laughed. " They will not be confined to the nursery floor for the next two weeks while the adults have the run of the park in which to enjoy a carefree, child-free existence," she said. "Wulfric and I decided with our very first child that we would enjoy our family to the full before they grow up and take flight. Our children have the run of the house for much of the time. When other people visit us with their children, the same rule applies—or lack of a rule, if you will. A few of our guests may be dismayed, but they need not be. There are adults galore, not to mention nurses and governesses, to entertain the children and keep an eye on them. The noise may be deafening at times, but it can be ignored."

He liked the lady. She was certainly as unlike his image of a duchess as it was possible to be. It was difficult to see her as the wife of the austere, haughty Duke of Bewcastle with his cool silver eyes and ever-present quizzing glass. Bewcastle allowed his children to run riot about his house, did he? That would have to be seen to be believed.

"Robert," the duchess said, addressing the back of his son's head, which was buried against his neck, "you are almost six years old, are you not? You may be the very person I need. There is a four-year-old boy over there by the window who is looking very unhappy indeed because he knows no one and is too shy to make himself known. I fear he will not enjoy his stay here if someone a little older does not befriend him. Could that older boy possibly be you? It would be extremely kind of you though you must not feel obliged. His name is Tommy."

For a moment Robert did not respond. Then he lifted his head and looked across the crowded room to where a little ginger-haired boy was sitting on the window seat, playing forlornly with a small sailing ship.

"I'll come with you, Robbie, if you like," Georgette offered.

But Robert seemed not to hear her. He did not protest when Michael set him down. He set off across the room without taking his eyes off the other child and bent over him, his hands on his knees as he said something, just as though he were an octogenarian addressing an infant. Tommy tucked his chin against his chest before looking up and extending the hand holding the toy ship toward Robert, who looked closely at it, touched it, and said something. He sat beside Tommy, who was now gazing at him with the beginnings—surely—of hero worship.

"That was well done of you," Michael said. "He is abnormally shy."

"I can see that," the duchess said with a smile. "He needs someone younger than himself to protect. He will be fine, Lord Staunton. You must not worry. Ah, here comes Eleanor with Lizzie."

He looked toward the door to see a young girl, who was leading—or being led by—a black and white border collie on a short leash. His daughter shrieked before he had a chance to look at the woman who had entered the room with her.

"Miss Thompson!" Georgette cried—and dashed across the room.

And good God, it was indeed she. Miss Thompson. *Eleanor.*

"Your daughter knows my sister?" the duchess asked.

"We were stranded together at an inn yesterday," he said, gazing across the room. "Georgette escaped from her room and, before she was missed, talked Miss Thompson's head off in the dining room while she was having her tea. The lady is your sister? She was very kind to my daughter."

He was absurdly delighted to see her again and only very slightly embarrassed.

She was looking startled at Georgette's approaching figure, and then her eyes met his for one moment before his daughter hurled herself into her arms and almost bowled her over. He closed his eyes briefly.

The duchess laughed. "Do not discourage her enthusiasm," she said, correctly reading his expression. "There is sometimes a strange notion that perfect ladies ought to be demure and that girls ought to be brought up to aspire to such perfection."

Miss Thompson, having been released from Georgette's clutches, was introducing her to her young companion, who looked a few years older than his daughter.

"She is Lizzie," the duchess explained, "the Marquess of Attingsborough's daughter. The marchioness used to teach with Eleanor in Bath. The dog is Horace. He leads her about with only the occasional mishap. He has been trained since she first acquired him and he led her spectacularly astray one afternoon on the estate next to ours when there were at least a dozen of us adults supposedly keeping an eye on her."

Michael looked more closely. "She is blind?" he asked.

"Since birth," she said. "But sometimes one almost forgets. Claudia and Joseph give her all the rein she needs to explore her world, and Claudia has found a way of educating her so that she may live as rich a life as anyone else."

"It is not easy being a parent," he said with great lack of originality.

"It is not," she agreed, "and someone ought to warn us before we launch into the state with blissful ignorance. Shall we go down for tea before we are deafened, and take Eleanor with us?"

"Papa," Georgette shrieked as they approached the door. "Miss Thompson is here. Is it not the *best* surprise *ever*? And this is Lizzie, and her dog is Horace and goes everywhere with her because she is blind and he acts as her eyes. Is that not clever? I am going to ask her a million questions about being blind. I have never met a blind person before."

Michael winced, but Lizzie only laughed. "Neither have I," she said. "Is that not funny? I have never met anyone else who is blind. Shall we go to my room, where it will be a little quieter?"

"Oh, yes, and perhaps we may be friends," Georgette said, and off they went, arm in arm, the dog trotting beside his mistress.

Robert was engrossed with the ship, which he and Tommy were sailing on the seat between them, their heads almost touching above it.

"Miss Thompson." Michael smiled at the lady. "You told me you were on your way to spend the summer with your family. I told you I was on my way to a house party. Neither of us mentioned any names or places, though, did we? I am delighted to see you again, and I think it possible my daughter is quite pleased too though you may not have noticed."

She laughed and...blushed? "I am delighted too," she said. "Has Lord Staunton told you we found ourselves marooned at the same inn last night, Christine? He was kind enough to invite me to dine with him in the only private parlor available."

Michael offered them each an arm and they made their way downstairs. He was still smiling when they stepped into the crowded drawing room a couple of minutes later. Perhaps he had done the right thing after all in coming here. And really it had not felt awkward at all meeting Miss Thompson again. He had refined too much on that accidental kiss and the attraction he had felt for her toward the end of last evening.

And then his eyes alit upon two fashionably dressed ladies across the room, the younger looking very fetching indeed in a pale primrose afternoon dress.

Lady Connaught and Miss Everly.

Good God!

His smile faded.

* * * * *

Lindsey Hall could accommodate a vast number of guests and had done so on several occasions since Christine married the Duke of Bewcastle. Wulfric's three brothers and two sisters were here with their spouses and growing families. So was all of Christine's family. And there were several other guests, relatives, and friends. She had invited the Earl of Staunton, Christine explained to Eleanor and Hazel and their mother while they were sitting over their coffee in the cozy sitting room next to Mrs. Thompson's bedchamber the following morning, because he had kind eyes and she had heard he brought his children with him to London each spring and devoted much of his free time to them, taking them to places that would interest and entertain them.

"But it sounded to me," she said, "as though the children were not often in the company of others, and that made me sad. Sad for them and sad for him, for I believe he dotes on them. I have been told he doted on his late wife too, though I never knew her."

"Poor gentleman," their mother said.

Christine had not planned activities for every moment of the two weeks. Everyone must feel free to relax and enjoy the summer in good company, she had explained at dinner last evening. Everyone must come and go as they pleased and not feel obliged to do anything they would rather avoid.

They did tend to move about in crowds, however. On the first afternoon, which was hot and sunny with not a cloud in the sky, someone—Christine? The Marchioness of Hallmere, the former Lady Freyja Bedwyn, Wulfric's sister?—had suggested going out to the hill that descended in a long, wide slope from the wilderness walk almost to the bank of the lake, and children and adults flocked there in the most exuberant of spirits though no one had explained what was so delightful about a long, steep hill.

Eleanor doubted Wulfric had opened his home to many house parties before he met her sister, and she had never observed him either to romp or to frolic since then, or even to bend sufficiently to smile and relax and look as though he were enjoying himself. But, observing him as she walked from the house to discover what the excitement was all about, it seemed to her that he was happy. He was standing at the foot of the hill, his hands clasped behind his back, his booted feet slightly apart, an austere expression on his face, watching excited, shrieking children, including two of his own, rolling down the hill from the very top.

The person he was really watching, though, Eleanor saw as she came up to him, was Christine, who was hurtling downward, her body straight, her arms stretched above her head, her dress bunched up about her knees, shrieking. She was not the only adult thus engaged. Freyja and two of her brothers, Lord Alleyne Bedwyn and Lord Rannulf Bedwyn, were also part of the action, to the huge amusement of their own children and other people's.

"Why could I not have married one of the respectable Thompson sisters?" Wulfric asked without turning his head.

Eleanor laughed. "Because Hazel was already married and I would not have had you even if you had asked," she said.

"That is very deflating to my self-esteem," he told her.

"That *even if you had asked* is a key point, Wulfric," she said. "Only Christine would do for you. Admit it. And it was because she is as she is."

Robert Benning, she was delighted see, was leading the younger, red-haired child with whom he had been playing in the nursery yesterday up the hill by the hand. He was bent slightly toward him, like a parent protecting his chick. And, interestingly, another infant caught up to them up as Eleanor watched—he was Jules, son of Gervase, the Earl of Rosthorn's son, Wulfric's nephew—and took Robert's other hand, no doubt seeing in him an older boy who was a rock of stability. Georgette too was trudging up the hill with Lizzie and the girl's father and talking animatedly to both of them.

"Quite so," Wulfric said, watching as Christine caught a little girl at the bottom of the hill and swung her about in a high circle, laughing and whooping up at her. The Countess of Rosthorn, the former Lady Morgan Bedwyn, Wulfric's youngest sibling, was doing much the same thing a short distance away with young Miranda Bedwyn, Lord Rannulf's daughter. "You are looking…

subdued, Eleanor."

Oh, gracious. Was she? But those unblinking silver eyes of his, so disconcerting to many people, did not miss much. He turned them upon her now—appropriately enough, his eyes were like a wolf's.

"Because I am not risking life and limb by rolling down the hill?" she asked, laughing again.

He was not to be deterred, "What is troubling you?" he asked.

"Absolutely nothing at all," she said, "beyond a little weariness after a busy term."

All about them in the warm sunshine house guests of all ages were at play. Even those who were not laboring up the hill in order to tumble down it were watching those who were and calling out comments and encouragement and laughing and whistling and applauding and, in a few cases, tending bumps and bruises and soothing tears. But the Duke of Bewcastle's austere attention was focused fully upon his sister-in-law.

"You are not as happy," he said, "as you expected to be." It was not a question.

"Oh, I love my school," she protested, quite truthfully, "and I love my fellow teachers, every one of whom has both the skill and the enthusiasm and understanding I expect of them. I love my girls, from the haughtiest and most obnoxious of the wealthy ones to the cattiest and most belligerent of the charity cases. I love what I do. It *matters*."

"But?" He raised one eloquent eyebrow.

She sighed. "But—"

"Bewcastle," a strident voice said, and Lady Connaught sailed up beside them, dressed in all the splendor she might have worn on Bond Street in London or on a drive in Hyde Park at the fashionable hour of the afternoon. Plumes nodded above the flower-trimmed brim of her large bonnet. Her daughter was with her, dressed as though for a garden party in Richmond, her arm drawn through the Earl of Staunton's. "How delightful it is to see all the dear children enjoying themselves, though I am surprised you would allow them to expose themselves to such danger. I am surprised too that the mothers of the girls would allow them to behave more like ill-bred hoydens than the young ladies they must aspire to be when they grow older. I am surprised you did not send them with their nurses somewhere not quite so close to the house. Their shrieks were audible as soon as we stepped out of doors."

Wulfric was suddenly all cool hauteur. His quizzing glass was in his hand and raised halfway to his eye.

"Are you surprised, ma'am?" he asked. "If there is indeed danger, it is slight and there are many doting parents on hand to deal with scraped knees and bumped noses. In my experience, exuberant girls often grow up to be perfectly delightful and well-bred ladies. My sisters are a case in point, as is Her Grace.

And why, on a summer day, when the children are having a great deal of fun, should the pleasure of watching them and listening to them and even, in some cases, of joining in their games be reserved for their nurses? It would not seem quite fair."

What was also not quite fair, Eleanor thought with the greatest satisfaction, was that no one could ever argue with Wulfric—except Christine. Lady Connaught retreated into a dignified silence.

Eleanor's eyes met the Earl of Staunton's. She had recognized Miss Everly's name as soon as she had heard it yesterday, and Lady Connaught's too. The impression she had gained at the inn during dinner that he was courting Miss Everly had been quite correct. She was exquisitely lovely, and she seemed to be all sweetness and dimpled good nature. Eleanor had not warmed to her. There was something about her sweetness and something about her smile... Could it be that she was just a little jealous, Eleanor had asked herself yesterday and asked herself again now. How very ridiculous of her. She felt more than ever ashamed of that near-sleepless night while she relived a kiss that had not been a real kiss at all.

He looked back at her with expressionless eyes.

"Perhaps, ma'am," Wulfric was saying, "I may escort you back to the house and have tea and scones brought out onto the terrace. It will be quieter there. I believe my mother-in-law plans to sit there in the shade with a few of my other guests."

But she did not avail herself of his offer. Instead she turned her attention upon Eleanor. "I would be obliged if Miss Thompson would take a walk along the lakeshore with us," she said.

Eleanor looked at her in surprise. She had thought herself beneath the notice of such a grand lady. "Thank you. That would be pleasant," she lied.

"It must be very gratifying for you, Miss Thompson," Lady Connaught said as the four of them moved off, "that your sister succeeded in snaring England's greatest matrimonial prize a few years ago. It is a feather in your cap to be able to boast of the Duke of Bewcastle as your brother-in-law."

"Indeed it is, ma'am," Eleanor said. "I am delighted to boast of both my brothers-in-law because they make my sisters as happy as my sisters make them."

"It must be a matter of regret to you," Lady Connaught said, "that you were unable to do as well for yourself. However, your loss is possibly our gain. You own and manage a girls' school in Bath, I understand."

"I do indeed," Eleanor said and glanced at the earl. She had not told him that when they dined, only that she was a teacher. He smiled at her, and her breath caught annoyingly in her throat.

Lady Connaught drew breath to say more, but they were interrupted by Georgette, who had come dashing from the bottom of the hill to hurl herself upon Eleanor, just as she had done in the nursery yesterday. Her dress was strewn with assorted debris and streaked with grass stains. Her hair, still tied precariously behind her head was nevertheless disheveled and liberally decorated with grass and twigs. There was a dirt streak and a slight scratch across one of her cheeks. Her hands were dirty. Her eyes sparkled. And her mouth was, of course, in motion.

"Miss Thompson," she cried, "did you see? Did you, Papa? I just rolled down the hill for the sixth time. It looks ever so frightening from the top, but it is the best fun ever. Lizzie has come with me three times though the first time her papa had to come too. You see? There is her mama hugging her and her dog licking her hand. She is blind. Did you know that? But of course you did. You were with her yesterday. She is full of pluck, is she not? And Robbie—have you seen Robbie? Have you, Papa? Look, he is getting ready to roll down again. It was positively *inspired* of the duchess to send him to look after Tommy yesterday, was it not, for now he has a whole group of the very little ones thinking he is very grown up and wanting to be his friends. He has hardly glanced at me all afternoon. Oh, here he comes. Does it not do your heart good, Papa?"

While she had been speaking, she had caught Eleanor's hand in one of hers and reached out to take her father's hand in her other. She was almost jumping up and down between them now and laughing as Robert led his little band down the hill.

"It does indeed," the earl said. "I am very happy, Georgette, that you are both enjoying yourselves so much. I will be happier still when you recover your manners from wherever you have put them and make your curtsy to Lady Connaught and Miss Everly."

"Oh." She bobbed a curtsy that encompassed them both.

"Dear Lady Georgette," Miss Everly murmured. Her arm had been somehow forced from her escort's.

"It is perhaps a good thing you have no mama at the moment, Georgette," Lady Connaught said, smiling graciously. "She would doubtless be ashamed to own you."

All the light went out of the child, and her hold on Eleanor's hand slackened. "My mama would never *ever* have been ashamed of me," she said almost in a whisper.

"That is because she would have trained you to behave like a proper lady," Miss Everly said sweetly. "And then she would have been proud of you."

"I—" Georgette began.

"I believe Lizzie is waiting for you, Georgette," the earl said. "Go and have fun with her and the other children."

The child looked from him to Eleanor, her light still dimmed, her eyes glistening with what might be tears. Eleanor smiled.

"I am envious, I must confess," she said. "The duchess, my sister, has the courage to come rolling down that long hill, but I am afraid I would stand cowering at the top and then make some excuse to descend the sedate way along the wilderness path."

"I am proud that my daughter has more courage," the earl said, also smiling. "Off you go, Georgette. And try to leave at least some grass on the hill, will you?"

She released their hands at last, after looking earnestly at them each in turn and went dashing off to rejoin her new friend.

"Miss Thompson," Lady Connaught said "perhaps you can understand why Lord Staunton is in desperate need of your services—if, that is, your school is sufficiently strict with girls who are difficult."

The lady's interest in her was explained. Eleanor was the one who was to take the Earl of Staunton's precocious daughter off his hands so that Miss Everly as his new wife would not be troubled by her. No doubt there were other plans forming for Robert's future. Oh, it was none of her business, Eleanor thought as they moved onward. Except that she was being drawn into the scheme, which might just possibly be the best option for Georgette anyway if her father really did marry Miss Everly. Oh, was he *mad?*

"I would not describe Georgette as difficult, ma'am," the Earl of Staunton said, "only as having a greater than usual exuberance of spirit and an insatiable curiosity about the world around her."

"Almost all girls are difficult," Eleanor said, drawing his reproachful glance her way. "Growing up is difficult. At my school I always find myself more concerned about the girls who are *not* difficult. I try to discover what is wrong with them. As for strictness, well, it is a word that can be defined many ways. We do try, my teachers and I, to keep harsh punishments to a minimum, experience having taught us that they do not often have any permanent effect for the good. On the other hand, for our own peace of mind and for the wellbeing of our girls, we cannot allow anarchy. *Teaching* is difficult and perhaps one of the most enjoyable and rewarding of careers."

The walk did not last long. Neither Lady Connaught nor her daughter seemed to find her worth knowing after all, Eleanor thought with some amusement—or with what would have been amusement if she had not been feeling half sick with apprehension for those poor children.

And if she had not wanted to shake their papa until his teeth rattled.

CHAPTER 5

For his children's sake he was glad he had come, Michael decided after the first week of the house party. They were having the time of their lives. Georgette had become firm friends with Lizzie and Becky, Lord Aidan Bedwyn's adopted daughter, and a few of the other older girls. And she was free to pursue those friendships and be a carefree child of ten, for Robert did not need her constant protection. Oh, he still ran for cover if any adult or older child showed signs of singling him out for attention, but he had gathered about him a small circle of younger children who looked upon him as a leader, and he frolicked all day long with them. Sometimes, though, he needed an adult to observe some feat he was about to perform—floating on the lake without anyone holding him, for example—or to look at something he had found—a ladybird cupped in his palms, perhaps—and then he called out to Miss Thompson as well as to his papa. Once, when everyone was returning from a picnic after a few hours of vigorous play at the far side of the lake and he was tired, Robert took her hand almost absently, it seemed, and walked all the way back to the house with her, just as he might have done with his mother, had she lived.

Michael might have been enjoying the house party with unalloyed pleasure on his own account too if it were not for one fact. The house was comfortable, the park surrounding it spacious, the weather perfect, the company congenial, the activities varied. He had always considered the Bedwyns to be a haughty family, aloof and formidable, even cold. But when thrown into their company as he had been during the past week, he had discovered their more human side and actually liked them. They had forceful personalities and boundless energy, but they all, with the possible exception of Bewcastle himself, had a strong sense of fun too. They all appeared to have contracted happy marriages and adored their children and one another's—and the children of all the other guests too. And even Bewcastle, Michael was interested to discover, was deeply involved in a love match with his unlikely duchess and gazed upon their children in unguarded moments with a certain light in his silver eyes that proclaimed his love for them.

The one fact that marred Michael's pleasure was that he must have given the inadvertent impression in London that he was formally courting Miss Everly. She and her mother appeared to have been invited here upon the strength of that impression since he could not fathom any other reason why they were here. And they were being seen as a couple. Several times another guest had vacated the seat next to him in order to make room for Miss Everly or had stood aside outdoors to allow her to take his arm. Good manners prevented him from spurning her—but why should he anyway? He had liked her early in the Season, had singled her out for some attention, though no more than he had done with a few other young ladies. But he very much feared he was being maneuvered into making an offer he really did not wish to make.

Would he be feeling as disconcerted, he wondered, if he had not met Miss Thompson and if it had not become apparent to him that she was far more suited to caring for his children than a young chit not long out of the schoolroom and still very much under the thumb of a domineering and ambitious mother? And if it had not occurred to him that even apart from his children's needs he might be more comfortable with a woman closer to him in age?

He was thinking altogether too often about Eleanor Thompson. He found himself looking about for her during the day and feeling disappointed if he could not see her and far too aware of her when he could. It was entirely his own doing. She did absolutely nothing to attract his attention or seek him out. He had exchanged scarcely a word with her since that ghastly walk by the lake a week ago. When they had spoken, it had been almost exclusively in the presence of his children, whom she treated with great kindness and patience despite her claim that she was not good with youngsters.

And there were her smiling eyes and the faint laugh lines at their corners, and her quiet, dignified demeanor and understated elegance and… Dash it all, he liked her, yet he felt guilty whenever he felt drawn to seek out her company, as though he were being unfaithful to Miss Everly—a thoroughly ridiculous thought. He had not in any way committed himself to the girl. He had not invited her here. And he deeply resented what Lady Connaught had tried to do that afternoon when she had invited first him and then Miss Thompson to walk with them. He was furious at the memory of her telling Georgette that Annette would have been ashamed of her.

The matter came to a crisis one afternoon when almost everyone was gathered out on the wide lawn to the west of the house, some sitting, others strolling, a large group playing a spirited game of cricket. The duchess was playing a circle game with an army of toddlers, something that involved joined hands and a lot of chanting and falling down with shrieks of merriment. Michael had been talking for a while with Lord Rannulf Bedwyn and the Countess of Rosthorn, his sister, and with Kit Butler, Viscount Ravensberg, an acquaintance of his, and Kit's wife, who had come over with their children from Alvesley, the neighboring estate. He left them in order to watch Robert, who was on one of the cricket teams with two of his young friends. Miss Thompson was strolling some distance away with Bewcastle. He looked around for Georgette. She was not with either Lizzie or Becky. Becky was up to bat at cricket and Lizzie was sitting on the grass close to her mother and father, rocking her sleeping baby brother in her arms.

And then he spotted her. She was seated cross-legged—*cross-legged, Georgette?*—on the grass looking up at Lady Connaught and Miss Everly, who occupied two of the comfortable chairs that had been carried from the house. His first reaction was alarm for her, but she did not look either trapped or sullen. Nor was she silently listening. She was talking animatedly and looking rather pleased with herself. What the devil? He hurried in their direction.

"Yes," she was saying, "she is going to be our new mama, and Robbie and I can hardly wait. We love her a whole heap."

A whole heap?

"Indeed?" Lady Connaught injected a world of meaning into the one word. "And are we to expect a betrothal announcement any time soon?"

"Oh," Georgette said, smiling sunnily, "he has not asked her yet. He is waiting for the right moment. But it is just a matter of—" But she had spotted him, and what she had been about to say went forever unspoken. She greeted him with that wide smile of hers in recognition of the fact that she knew she was in Big Trouble. "Oh, there you are, Papa."

"Here I am," he agreed. "And poor Nurse would need a heavy dose of smelling salts if she were to see you sitting that way for the whole world to see."

"Oh, not the whole world, Papa," she said, scrambling nevertheless to her feet and smoothing out her dress. "I must go and find Lizzie. Oh, there she is with the baby. I shall go and hold him for a while. Her mama and papa will let me." And off she went, leaving disaster behind her—or a colossal embarrassment at the very least.

"I understand," Lady Connaught said with awful civility while her daughter looked down at her hands in her lap and smoothed out the glove on one hand with the fingers of the other, "that congratulations are soon to be in order, Lord Staunton."

He stood looking down at them, his hands clasped at his back. They were a little apart from everyone else, having had their chairs moved into the shade of an old oak tree. They always seemed to be a little apart from everyone else.

"I heard only the tail end of what my daughter had to say," he said. "I would be interested to know the identity of the new mama she believes she is about to have." Though he suspected he knew the answer.

"Miss Eleanor Thompson," she said, "who has acquired ideas above her station, even if her sister was clever enough to reel in a duke for herself."

"I believe, ma'am," he said, "Miss Thompson would be as surprised to hear the news as I am."

She looked hard at him while Miss Everly changed hands to smooth out the other glove. "Perhaps, Lord Staunton," Lady Connaught said, "it is time for *some* announcement to be made. Or perhaps it is in your nature to procrastinate. You still seem not to have made up your mind to send your daughter to a school where her shocking behavior will be taken in hand before it is too late. And you still have not taken the step the whole of the beau monde has been expecting any time since Easter. I am a patient woman, but where my daughter is concerned my patience has its limits."

And Michael knew in a flash that his conscience was clear. Yes, he had singled out Miss Everly during the Season, but never to such a marked degree that his interest would be generally seen as a courtship. Several times when they had been in the same theater or picnic party it had been none of his doing, just as the fact that they were together here had had nothing to do with him. He had admired the young lady, he had even considered her as a possible wife, but he had never come even close to declaring himself or compromising her. He had never been alone with her and had never so much as kissed the back of her hand if memory served him correctly. Rather, he had been pursued, persistently and relentlessly. He glanced at Miss Everly, who was looking off toward the cricket game, an expression of faint scorn on her face.

"Miss Everly is fortunate to have a parent so devoted to her wellbeing, ma'am," he said. "As a parent myself I can well understand. Giving due consideration to decisions that will affect the whole of the future of one's child is not procrastination in my vocabulary, however. My dearest wish is to do the right thing for the future happiness of both my children, but it is not always easy to know just what that right thing is. Until I do know, I will not act. As for any expectations the *ton* may have of me, ma'am, I do not know what they might be and do not normally allow my actions to be dictated by others anyway. I am a widower with two children, and those children's happiness must always come first with me, even before my own inclination if there should ever be a conflict. Fortunately, I do not believe that has happened yet."

"I believe, Lord Staunton," Lady Connaught said, "you have made yourself perfectly clear. My daughter has been much in demand this year. After this house party is over, we will be on our way to that of the Marchioness of Borgland. Her son the marquess—his father died two years ago, you may recall—made a special request of her that we be invited. I believe it will be a more exclusive and refined gathering than this, with children—if there are any—confined very correctly to the schoolroom and the care of their nurses. We accepted the invitation here only because the Duchess of Bewcastle was insistent, but her humble origins have been apparent all week, have they not? There has been much that has bordered upon vulgarity. One can only pity the poor duke."

Robert was still in the thick of the cricket crowd, Michael saw at a quick glance, and Georgette was seated on the grass beside Lizzie, Attingsborough's baby, now awake, on her lap. He had a fistful of her hair in his chubby hand and she was grimacing and laughing. Miss Thompson and Bewcastle were back from their walk and were making directly this way. Michael stood aside to include them in the group.

"Ma'am, Miss Everly," Bewcastle said, addressing both ladies, "it has ever been my observation that young children are able to express their exuberance only in shrill shrieks and squeals. It is remarkably gracious of you to have come out here with the rest of the company to have your ears murdered. Have you attempted the wilderness walk yet? It is not as arduous as it may look, and it offers a number of very pleasing prospects and a measure of peace and quiet. It would be my pleasure to show it to you."

Bewcastle never joined in play, Michael had noticed during the week, as his brothers and sisters all did on occasion, but he was ever the perfect host, unerringly singling out for attention any guest who was for some reason not part of a larger group. Lady Connaught, clearly gratified, rose to her feet and took his arm. He offered his other to Miss Everly and they set off for the wilderness path. Miss Thompson turned away.

"Miss Thompson," Michael called after her. She stopped and turned to look at him, and he felt a sudden lifting of his spirits at the realization that a great burden had just been taken from his shoulders. "Your brother-in-law had a point, did he not?" He grimaced as someone hit the cricket ball with a loud crack, sending it high and long, and the batter's team and its supporters whistled and cheered wildly. "The noise is deafening. Would you care for a stroll about the lake?"

Perhaps she would not care for any such thing. She had just returned from a walk with Bewcastle and might be longing to sit down. She did not answer immediately. But then her lips curved into a smile.

"Yes. Thank you," she said, and he offered his arm.

* * * * *

Wulfric had been in no hurry all week to renew his interrupted conversation with Eleanor. Neither had she. It would be better to leave it, she had decided, until after the house party was over. But today, when almost everyone was settled on the west lawn enjoying the sunshine and the games and one another's company, he had suggested a stroll before leading her far enough from the company to ensure some uninterrupted conversation.

"I believe your final word was *but*," he said and she looked at him and laughed. "You had finished making an impassioned protestation of love for your school and everything and everyone within its walls. You had assured me that what you do matters. And then came the *but* a mere moment before we were interrupted. One might call you the mistress of suspense."

"Your memory is all too acute, Wulfric," she said.

"Continue where you left off, if you please," he said. "There is a certain… sadness in you, Eleanor, that is of concern to Christine and therefore to me. What is it, my dear?"

She looked sharply at him. Wulfric was not usually lavish with endearments. And was it true that Christine was concerned about her?

"I fear I must disappoint you," she said. "I fear you will think me lacking in perseverance and a knowledge of what I want of life. I fear you will think me a failure."

"And does my opinion matter to you?" he asked.

She sighed. "And Mama's opinion and Hazel's and Charles's and Christine's too," she said. "But most of all yours because you have invested in me." Also because despite herself she was a little afraid of him, as she suspected all people were except her sister.

"You had better tell me," he said.

"All that I told you about my school and the teachers and the girls is true," she told him. "But…it was a mistake to take over so impulsively from Claudia when she married the Marquess of Attingsborough. There, I have said it. I do not enjoy the administration, the business, the responsibility, the…loneliness. And I have been so endlessly *tired*. And yes, unhappy. I made a mistake, but you believed in me and made it happen for me with your loan."

Purchasing the school was not the only mistake she had made, she feared. She had botched the whole of her adult life since Gregory's death. She had prided herself upon being the one woman who would be steadfast in her grief over the loss of the love of her life. She had lived by that decision even after the rawness of grief had passed and even its gentler melancholy aftermath. Sometimes she had had to whip up her memories. Sometimes she had not thought of him for days, even perhaps weeks at a time. Sometimes she could not remember either his face or his voice. In the meanwhile she had lost her youth, her chance to find someone else for whom she might feel an affection even if not the passion of her young love, her chance to marry and have children of her own. She had been proud of her devotion to a memory. Yet now her fight against loneliness was almost constant. Her fortieth birthday was creeping up with very little to show for all the years. And now she had fallen in love again—with a man who was probably about to marry a young lady quite unworthy of him.

"It was a gift," Wulfric said. "And I neither regret giving it nor blame you, Eleanor. Sometimes our dreams lead us in the wrong direction and it would be foolish to continue pursuing them out of sheer stubbornness or the fear of disappointing others. There are other dreams waiting to be dreamed—the right dreams, the ones that will lead to contentment."

She turned her head to look at him in some surprise. She had never heard him talk thus before.

He met her gaze. "I am a happy man, Eleanor," he said. "I want your happiness too, not your fear of disappointing me. You surely cannot doubt that your mother and sisters too want nothing but your happiness."

She drew a slow breath. "I have a potential buyer," she said. "If I sell, I will repay your *loan*, Wulfric, though I will not insult you by offering any interest on it."

"And what will you do then?" he asked. "Will the new owner wish to keep you on staff as a teacher?"

She had been keeping her mind away from that question. She was not sure of the answer. She was not even sure she would be able to recapture the pleasure she had felt as a simple teacher at the school.

"I do not know," she said.

"Your mother and Christine would be ecstatic to have you live here," he said. "It would please me too."

"Thank you," she said. "Wulfric, I am so *sorry*. I feel so…defeated."

"Only you can wrestle with that demon," he said. They had been making their way back gradually to where everyone else was thronged. "Christine is wrestling with a couple of her own. She was neatly maneuvered into inviting Lady Connaught and her daughter here, but she swears she would have resisted to the death had she not believed Staunton was courting the daughter. Is it as clear to your eye as it is to Christine's and mine that he is trying desperately not to do so but is perhaps too much the gentleman to be firm with them? The mother is appalling, is she not? One can only hope that the man the daughter eventually marries will be capable of tearing his wife—and himself—from her pernicious influence. However, while they are at my home they must be treated as welcome and valued guests. Will the wilderness walk be too much for them, do you think?"

Was it as clear to her eye? Perhaps her eye had been clouded by her anxiety for the future of the Earl of Staunton's children. Oh, and by her own inappropriate feelings for him. One might as well be honest at least within the confines of one's own mind. *Was* he trying to avoid Miss Everly?

"Not if you escort them there," she said. "They will see it as an acknowledgement of their superiority over all your other guests."

"Quite so," he agreed, and a few minutes later he was leading them away, one lady on each arm, and Eleanor was moving off in some confusion when she realized she had been left alone with the Earl of Staunton, slightly removed from everyone else.

"Miss Thompson," he said, stopping her. And oh, she knew as she looked back at him that she was doing exactly what Wulfric had just suggested she do. She was dreaming another dream. Very foolishly. Very unwisely. Unfortunately, however, dreams seemed to be beyond the control of the rational mind.

Soon she was strolling away from the crowd yet again, toward the lake this time and on the arm of the Earl of Staunton.

CHAPTER 6

"My children have taken a liking to you," he said as he turned their steps in the direction of the lake. "I hope they have not been making a nuisance of themselves." And he fervently hoped Georgette had not told her, as she had Lady Connaught and Miss Everly, that she was to be their new mama, that it was only a matter of time before he got around to asking her.

"I have been touched," she said. "Although I love young children, I have never considered myself good with them as my sisters are."

"But I daresay," he said, "they have never been as good with older children as you are."

"You are kind," she said. "Your son is enjoying himself, is he not? Has he never had children younger than himself with whom to play?"

"All his cousins and all the children of our closest neighbors are older," he said. "Young Tommy was a godsend. He and a few other infants see Robert as an older, bolder boy who will condescend to play with them. And I believe he is seeing himself through their eyes."

"Yesterday," she said, "when several of us climbed the tower folly on the wilderness walk, he took my hand to help me up the winding stairs and then pointed out for my edification all the landmarks we could see from the top."

He wondered why she had never married. Had it been from choice? From lack of opportunity? From an unwillingness to marry just anyone in order not to end up a spinster? Had she held out for love or some other ideal that had never happened for her?

"I am sorry," he said, "for that encounter with Lady Connaught last week. She treated you as an inferior who might be of service to her. I am glad you put her in her place. "

"Did I?" She turned her head to look at him but did not speak. They were crossing the driveway before the large circular flower bed and stopped to look up at the fountain. Lord Aidan Bedwyn had explained to him how it worked so that it could shoot water so high. It was a quite ingenious mechanism.

"I have almost made up my mind," he said, "not to send Georgette away to school. Not yet, anyway, and never just because it would be more convenient to me to have her out of the way. I shall ponder the matter carefully over the next year or two, and I shall consult her wishes. She has had a governess since she was six, though I fear she outstripped her teacher in academic knowledge some time ago and was never much influenced by her in other ways. Fortunately, the lady resigned in London a month or so ago in order to marry a barrister. I will seek another governess, one who can teach both children and somehow serve all their educational needs. It will not be easy to find such a paragon."

"I may be able to help you," she said. "My school always takes in a certain number of charity girls. Part of my responsibility at the end of their schooling is to find them suitable employment. I never turn them out into the world until I am satisfied that they will be happily settled. There is one girl I have been unable to place yet. She is too intelligent and too…oh, talented and full of energy to fit any of the offers that have been made. I have even thought of keeping her on at the school as an assistant instructor until there is an opening for a regular teacher, but…well, I may not be able to do that after all." She did not explain.

"Thank you," he said. "If she comes recommended by you, then I am satisfied. *She* may not be satisfied, of course, if and when she meets Georgette."

She smiled and changed the subject. "I am always disappointed," she said, "if I come here to find that the waterfall has been turned off, as it is in the winter. It seems to characterize Lindsey Hall. It has grandeur but brightness and fluidity too. Alleyne Bedwyn once told me that when he was suffering from memory loss after receiving a head wound at Waterloo it was the fountain that kept flashing into his mind when all else was blank."

They gazed at the water together and listened to the rushing, soothing sound of it.

"Are you happy?" he found himself asking her and then could have bitten out his tongue. Where had that question come from?

She did not answer for a while and he wondered if she would. He was on the verge of apologizing for the question.

"I have everything I could possibly want," she said. "I have employment that I have enjoyed. It has brought me a sense of worth and has brought me into company with adults and young girls whom I esteem and even love. I have a family I love dearly."

She had not quite answered his question, he thought. Or perhaps she had. Perhaps being independent, doing what she loved and what was important to her had brought her happiness.

"And you?" she asked him. "Are you happy? But you spoke somewhat on the subject when we dined together."

"I had a happy marriage, which was all too brief," he said. "Now I have my home, my friends, and my children. I am well blessed. And at last I am open to future happiness. I have concluded that it is not disloyal to the dead to live on."

She turned her head to look almost fiercely at him. "Oh," she said, "you are so very right."

Their eyes met and locked. And there was a pause in the conversation, charged with something unidentifiable while a flush rose to her cheeks. And he asked the unpardonable question.

"Why have you never married?" he asked her.

They were strolling beside the lake, the wilderness walk above them, trees just ahead of them to offer seclusion from company and shade from the sun. Off to one side, beyond the end of the walk, was a round stone building that looked like a dovecote.

She smiled faintly and lowered her eyes. "Perhaps," she said, "because I was too much of a romantic. I was betrothed once upon a long time ago to a cavalry officer. I was head over heels in love with him. No one had ever loved as we loved. Had I been a poet, I would doubtless have filled volumes with flowery verse pulsing with emotion. Though I must not make light of what was very real. He was killed in Spain at the Battle of Talavera, and I really did not expect to live on myself. Or want to. If I could have died of grief, I would gladly have done so—not out of any poetic ideal of sentimental grief but because it was really too painful to be borne. Alas, I could not die. But I would not love again. How could I? The only love of my life was gone forever. Grieving, remaining true to his memory, became a habit with me, a habit I have always thought to be a virtue until recently. But my devotion has not made any difference to him, has it? He has been dead all this time."

They had stopped walking, as though by mutual consent. They were among the trees, though in a grassy clearing. The water here was dark green as it reflected the leaves on the trees. One tree was bent toward the water, a stout branch reaching out over it, and it struck Michael that it would be a daring boy's dream as a diving platform. And a girl's too, he added mentally, thinking of Georgette. An invisible bird was trilling from somewhere among the trees. A distant swell of cheering from the direction of the cricket pitch only accentuated the peace that surrounded them.

"How lovely it is just here," she said. "It is very peaceful, is it not?"

"There is something about water and trees," he said, "that is soothing to the soul."

She turned her head to smile at him and he smiled back—before lowering his head to hers and kissing her. It seemed the most natural thing in the world, a gesture of shared pleasure in the moment and of affection too. When he moved his head back she was still half smiling, and her eyes gazed back into his without wavering. He touched the fingers of one hand to her cheek and moved them down to trace the line of her jaw to her chin.

"I am sorry," he said.

"Please do not be," she told him, her voice a mere whisper of sound.

And he gathered her into his arms and did what he had been dreaming of doing ever since that evening at the inn more than a week ago. He kissed her properly, as a man kisses a woman to whom he is sexually attracted. He parted his lips over hers while her own lips relaxed and her arms came about him, and he teased her lips until they parted and then stroked his tongue into her mouth, exploring its warm, moist depths. She suckled his tongue gently while his temperature rose and he moved his hands down the inward curve of her spine over the flaring of her hips to her bottom. She had a woman's figure rather than a girl's. He hardened into arousal and held her to him, not trying to disguise the fact. She made a sound deep in her throat and pressed closer. Heat flared between them.

He wondered just how secluded this place was. And he wondered if she was a virgin. And he remembered that at least three people were on the wilderness walk not far away and that his children and a host of other people were no great distance from where they were standing and embracing.

She smelled of something subtly and fragrantly feminine.

She was the one to break the embrace, though not hurriedly. She set her hands on his shoulders and moved slightly away from him.

"It is not at all the thing, is it?" she said, smiling apologetically. "I have just admitted to feeling regret over the lost years and to a certain loneliness. But I do not want to give you the wrong idea."

He did not ask what that wrong idea was. He regretted the end of the embrace, but at the same time he was relieved by it. He had just extricated himself from one entanglement. He did not want to land himself in another before he had had time to consider. He had known her for only a week, and during most of that time he had avoided her or she had avoided him. He was not sure which.

"We are in a beautiful place on a warm summer's day," he said, offering his arm and strolling onward with her, "and we are a man and a woman. I think we can be forgiven for a little harmless dalliance. Would you not agree?"

He wished he had chosen a different word. *Dalliance* sounded trivial, a little sordid.

"I would," she said.

"It is strange, is it not," he said, "how one arrives at adulthood believing that one's childhood and youth have been a journey leading to a fixed destination and a settled and lasting happiness. Happily-ever-after. It is only as one grows older that one realizes that nothing is static, that nothing is assured. All of us suffer the troubles of life sooner or later, no matter how carefully we have planned our lives."

"Ah, but life is not all troubles," she said. "There are delights too, pinnacle moments of extreme joy and longer spells of contentment. Perhaps we need both extremes so that we do not remain the shallow beings most of us are when we first grow up but develop depth of character and empathy with others. Perhaps we would not recognize or appreciate happiness if we did not also know unhappiness."

"Of course you are right." He looked at her and laughed. "And wise."

"This is one of those pinnacle moments," she said—and flushed.

Of extreme joy? Yes, all caution aside, it was.

"Yes," he said.

"And the future always holds endless possibilities," she said. "As Wulfric just observed, we can always dream new dreams to replace the old."

Bewcastle had said such a thing? It was hard to imagine. But Michael's preconceptions of the icy duke had been shaken a few times during the past week.

"And yet," he said, "I suppose most people dream of the same thing in essence—of love and happiness."

"Do we?" She turned her head, frowning slightly as though she were considering the truth of what he had said. "Are we—"

But he never heard what she was about to ask. They had walked almost completely about the lake by now.

"Papa, Papa-a-a, " a voice cried from ahead of them, and they both looked up to see Robert dashing and skipping toward them, exuberant excitement in every line of his body. "Georgie said she saw you come this way. Papa, I hit the ball. I hit it a great whack and that man with lots of hair and a big nose—*William's* papa—tried to catch it and almost did but dropped it. I scored a run."

He had wormed his way between them and was beaming up at Michael even as his hand found its way into Miss Thompson's.

"What a clever boy," Michael said, ruffling his son's fuzzy blond hair and blessing Lord Rannulf Bedwyn for deliberately fumbling the ball. "My son, the star cricketer. And then you abandoned your team?"

"I came to tell you," Robert said, quite unrepentant, and he beamed ecstatically from one to the other of them.

"I am glad you did," Michael said, smiling down into his face and feeling very close to tears.

"I came to tell you *both*," Robert said.

"Well, thank you," Miss Thompson said. "I am honored, Robert."

She was smiling at his son. And yes, Michael thought, taking the child's other hand in his own, he was filled to the brim with joy. She had been quite right about pinnacle moments. One must always be careful not to miss them.

* * * * *

Georgette and Robert shared a bedchamber with Mrs. Harris on the nursery floor. Although it was close to bedtime, however, they were both still in the main nursery, Georgette talking with Becky and Lizzie and Becky's older brother Davy, and Robert sitting in a huddle of small children over by the window, all of them listening intently while the red-haired Lady Rannulf Bedwyn read them a story. Michael seized the opportunity to send Georgette to the room while his son was otherwise occupied. There was a screech of laughter from the little ones as Lady Rannulf acted the part of one of the nasty, evil characters—she was, Michael had gathered, something of an actress.

Georgette was sitting cross-legged on her bed when he entered the room and nodded to Mrs. Harris to leave them for a few moments. He sat down on the edge of the bed and patted one of his daughter's knees. She favored him with one of her dazzling guilty smiles.

"Just a one-word, question," he said. "Why?"

"Why *what*, Papa?"

The smile turned to a wide-eyed innocent look, which disappeared when he merely waited quietly for her answer. He was surprised and not a little alarmed when tears welled into her eyes. This was not one of her usual tactics and was perhaps not a tactic at all. He waited nonetheless.

"They would send me away, Papa," she said. "I don't mind so much being sent to school. I might enjoy it though I think I would rather stay at home. But they would not really be sending me *to* school, Papa, but *away* from you and Robbie. And then they would insist that he be a proper boy like all others and that he stop sitting on your lap and cuddling up to you and lifting his face at night for you to kiss him. They told me how surprised they were that you allowed such unmanly behavior in your son and heir. And before you know it, they will be sending him away too to a school that will toughen him up, and we all know how boys get toughened up in the schools that are supposed to be for the education of gentlemen."

Good God!

"Georgie," he said, unconsciously using the shortened form of her name she had asked him two years ago to stop using, "do you really believe I would allow any lady—or her mother—to dictate to me what I do for and with my children? Do you really believe I would send either you or Robert *away* from me, to use your own emphasis?"

She stared at him with her tear-filled eyes. "She is beautiful, Papa," she said, "and I know gentlemen admire beautiful ladies and sometimes lose their wits over them."

Oh, Lord, where the devil had she heard that?

"I have a daughter and a son," he said. "I lost my wits to them when they were born, Georgette, and have not recovered them since. Nor do I wish to. Do you not know that you and Robert are all in all to me? Yes, I admire beautiful ladies, especially those who also have beautiful characters and like my children.

I may even marry one such lady one of these days. But only if I believe I can make her happy and make my children happy as well. I would never put my own happiness above yours and Robert's."

"I don't remember Mama very clearly," she said, "and Robbie does not remember her at all."

"I know," he said, patting her knee again. "She loved you both very, very much."

"I wish she hadn't had to die," she said.

"So do I, Georgie," he said.

"But since she had to," she said, "then I think you ought to have another wife, Papa, so that you will not be lonely any more. No, stop. I know you are going to say you aren't lonely, that Robbie and I are enough for you, but we aren't really enough. And I know you try to be a father and a mother to us, and you are the best papa *ever*. But you cannot be our mother too. We want a new one. And it is not because we don't love our real mama because we do. Forever and ever, Papa. But she can't be here with us, and we want someone who can be. We want a new mama. We have both looked for one. We have looked at home, and we looked in London, but we have never found the right one."

He would be bawling too if he was not careful, Michael thought, reaching across and scooping her up, all gangly arms and legs, to deposit on his lap. She was sniffing and scowling.

"Until now," she added defiantly, as though she expected he would reprimand her any moment. "We have found her, Papa, and we both want her. It's not just me, and it's not just Robbie. We both agree. But she cannot be our mama unless she is your wife and you have scarcely looked at her all week until you went walking with her this afternoon, and those other two have been trying to take your attention and trying to convince everyone else that you are practically *betrothed* to Miss Everly and pretty soon you will be whether you like it or not. And then you will have to marry her, and she will be your wife but she will never be our mama but we will have lost our chance to have one and in the meanwhile—"

"Georgie," he said firmly. "Stop, sweetheart. Take a breath."

She was fisting and unfisting her hands in her lap. She was gasping for breath.

"I am not going to marry Miss Everly," he told her. "I have made that clear to both her and Lady Connaught. And I will never marry anyone of whom you and Robert do not approve. But as for Miss Thompson, you know, I can make no promises. You can want her as a mama all you wish and I can want her as a wife all I wish, but if she does not want to have me as a husband and you and Robert as her children…well, there is nothing we can do about it, is there?"

She looked up at him, her eyes wide with incredulity. "Papa," she said, "you are the Earl of Staunton. You are rich. And you are handsome and nice and you have a lovely smile and you are not so very old. You could have any lady you want. I have seen the way ladies look at you. Do you seriously think you cannot make Miss Thompson love you and agree to marry you? The only thing that might make her *not* want you is me because I am Difficult and maybe Precocious and I talk a lot and ask endless questions because I want to know things. But I think she likes me anyway, so I am not a complete liability. Papa—"

He hugged her close and kissed the top of her head. "I want you to promise me something, Georgette," he said. "I want you to promise that you will not say a word to Miss Thompson about all this, about wanting her to be your mama. At best you may embarrass her. At worst you may distress her. She is an independent lady with a life of her own. She has a rich life in Bath and many responsibilities there. She owes us nothing. You must promise me."

He heard her sigh. "I promise," she said. "But, Papa, you must promise not to be a slow-top. We have only one more week here, and after that we may never see her again."

Fortunately Robert came into the room at that moment and jumped up onto the bed to snuggle close.

"Well?" Michael asked, setting an arm about him. "Are you enjoying yourself?"

"Mmm," Robert said and yawned hugely. "Tommy fell asleep in the middle of the last story and had to be carried to bed."

"Did he?" Michael said. "And you are going to be asleep pretty soon too. We had better get you undressed and tucked up in your bed before it happens."

* * * * *

Pinnacle moments of great joy were all very well while one was living them but not so wonderful when they were over, Eleanor thought over the next few days. Everything had come together to form perfection—the lovely setting by the lake, the warm summer weather, the easy conversation, the kiss. Ah, the kiss. It was her first for years and years. Indeed, she had only ever been kissed before by Gregory and that was so long ago that it seemed rather like something from another lifetime.

She would not refine too much upon this kiss, she decided as soon as she was alone again. It had flowed naturally from the occasion and was no indicator of undying love and an impending proposal of marriage. The very idea was ludicrous. She was a confirmed spinster of almost forty. She would not feel guilty about the kiss either. It was true that he must be considering marriage with Miss Everly. Christine had remarked in her hearing one day that she had invited the ladies because it appeared to be general knowledge that Miss Everly and the Earl of Staunton were a couple headed inevitably to the altar. But they were not officially betrothed yet, and Eleanor fervently hoped they never would be—entirely for the children's sake, of course. Oh, and for his sake too as she could not like Miss Everly and could not quite believe he would be happy with her.

Oh, and for your own sake too, Eleanor, she admitted to herself rather crossly. She could not bear the thought of him with someone as shallow as Miss Everly. Or with any other woman for that matter.

Eleanor avoided him as much as she could. She did not wish him to feel obligated in any way to her. She certainly did not want to give anyone the impression that she was pursuing him. Those cool silver eyes of Wulfric's rested speculatively upon her quite enough as it was, and Christine and Hazel did not miss much either.

The Earl of Staunton appeared to be avoiding her too. Certainly he made no further effort to single her out for walks or conversation. He played cricket and rowed on the lake. He played billiards and blind man's buff. He read the morning papers and stories to his children. He wrote letters and sat conversing with various groupings of adults. He went riding and fishing with a party of gentlemen and a few children. He turned pages of music at the pianoforte for one young lady and sang a duet with Hazel and laughed with her afterward over one ear-jarringly wrong note for which each assumed the blame. He went swimming and helped plan and direct a treasure hunt.

He was enjoying himself, Eleanor believed, and that indeed was the whole purpose of a country house party. He did not totally ignore her. He sat beside her a few times in the dining room and in groups that included her in the drawing room and out on the terrace. He fetched a book from the library that he had heard her say she wished to read. He chose to join her team for a spirited game of charades one evening and strolled over the wilderness walk with a group that included her one afternoon. He smiled whenever their eyes met and often had a word for her when they were close.

She felt slightly depressed and berated herself for being a fool.

To protect herself from further hurt yet without even realizing she was doing it, she adopted a manner of almost severe reserve whenever she was in his presence. She set her mind to other things. She wrote to Hortense Renney, the teacher who was interested in purchasing the school from her. Hortense was intelligent, well educated and well read, cheerful and energetic, and well liked by all. In her letter Eleanor did not mention staying on as a teacher. She would wait and see if Hortense suggested it and then decide if she would accept or not. They were friends, but Hortense might find the switch in their roles uncomfortable. So might she.

She did not know what she would do if the offer was not made or if she decided she could not stay. She tried to look upon her future as an exciting challenge. Provided she sold the school for a decent price, she would have a tidy nest egg left even after paying back Wulfric's loan.

She broke the news to her mother and sisters, none of whom was upset with her, only perhaps a little *for* her. All three assured her they would support her in whatever she decided to do. She told Claudia, the Marchioness of

Attingsborough, from whom she had purchased the school not so very long ago. Claudia was surprised and sympathetic and supportive—and hugged Eleanor warmly.

Wulfric's birthday was to be a day of busy celebration, though he had been heard to comment that only his wife would consider a fortieth birthday a cause for jollification. There was to be a children's outdoor party during the afternoon, weather permitting, a banquet early in the evening in the rarely used great medieval hall, and a grand dance in the ballroom to follow it.

Christine was in a great fever of activity and excitement during the morning, though there was no real need. Wulfric's secretary, his butler and housekeeper, and an army of servants had everything well in hand, Eleanor judged. Trying to lend a helping hand herself would only cause them all annoyance. Like the other guests, she stayed out of the way. She sat for a while in her mother's sitting room, but when it began to fill up with other ladies, she fetched a shawl from her room and went walking alone outside. She took a diagonal course across the wide lawn west of the house, no particular destination in mind. Servants and gardeners were setting up for the children's party in the area around the lake.

When she was some distance from the house, she became aware of a voice calling her name and turned to watch Robert Benning come dashing toward her, all alone. By the time he reached her he was breathless and wide-eyed, the blond fuzz of his hair even more unruly than usual. He stopped abruptly a few feet from her, hung his head, and scuffed the grass with the toe of his shoe, all his courage apparently having deserted him.

"Robert," Eleanor said, "what is it? Have you come to walk with me?" Her heart ached with love for the child, who shied away from every other adult except his father and his nurse.

He mumbled something.

"What?" she asked. She stooped down on her haunches to bring herself closer to his level. "Is something troubling you, sweetheart?"

"Georgie said I had to do it," he said, his chin still tucked against his chest. "Because she can't. She promised."

"And what is it you have to do?" she asked. This sounded very underhanded.

"Tell you," he said.

"Tell me?" She frowned. "What does she wish you to tell me?"

He mumbled something again and then looked abruptly up at her, his eyes huge and earnest. "That you are our mama," he blurted.

Eleanor tipped her head to one side. "I am your mama?"

"As soon as Georgie saw you," he said, "she knew. She told me to look for myself when you came for dinner, and then I knew too. And then we thought we would not see you again, but you were here and Georgie said it was fate and meant to be and all we had to do was let Papa know it too before he picked that other lady who is going to send Georgie away to school. Georgie told Papa, but he said you may not want to marry him or be our mama, and he made her promise not to tell you because it might embarrass you. But he hasn't done anything since then and in two days we are going home and will never see you again. Georgie said I must tell because a promise is a promise and she can't. But I think Papa will be cross with her for sending me instead. He will be cross with me too for coming. But I had to come, not just because Georgie said so. I don't want never to see you again. Please can you do something?"

Eleanor doubted he had ever strung together so many words in his life before. He was breathless and flushed and furiously kicking at the grass with one foot, and then he was rubbing both curled fists into his eyes and hanging his head again. She felt very close to tears. These two precious children wanted her for their mama? But their father did not want her for his wife?

"Papa said maybe you do not want to marry him and be our mama," Robert murmured into his chest, "because you have a life of your own and are someone important."

Eleanor reached out both arms and gathered him in. Ambiguous words, those—*maybe you do not want to marry him*. He had been avoiding being alone with her. But he had fetched her that book from the library. He had sat close to her a few times when he might have joined another group. She had been very careful on each occasion to be very correct and reserved in manner, lest he think she had foolish expectations. Was it possible...? And now that she thought of it, he had not spent much time with Miss Everly in the past few days.

"Robert, sweetheart," she said, "I cannot think of any greater honor than to be your mama and Georgette's. I love you both very dearly indeed. But it cannot happen, you know, unless I am also your papa's wife. And perhaps he does not want that. But if I cannot be your mama, I will always love you anyway." He was right, though. She would probably not see them again after they left here the day after tomorrow.

She stood up when he wriggled out of her embrace. "But you would if he *did* want it?" he asked her, his face all bright eagerness.

"Well, yes," she said, "but—"

She got no farther. He turned and darted away, running and skipping in the direction of the house.

"Oh," she said, reaching out one arm toward him. "But... Oh."

Oh, dear.

Oh, dear!

CHAPTER 7

Michael was playing billiards with a number of other guests who were staying out of the way of the preparations for the day's festivities. He was standing by one of the tables, cue in hand, when he felt something tapping persistently at the back of his waist. He turned to find his son standing there, looking up at him with a face that brimmed with excitement. He was supposed to be upstairs on the nursery floor with all the other children. But here he was and, wonder of wonders, he had walked into a room filled with adults.

"Papa," he cried as soon as he had his father's attention, "she said yes."

"Ah, one escaped convict," Lord Aidan Bedwyn said, smiling kindly down upon Robert who, surprisingly, did not duck for cover. It seemed doubtful he had even heard.

"Who said yes about what?" Michael asked.

"Miss Thompson did," Robert cried. "She said yes, she would like to be our mama, and she said she would be your wife too if you wanted."

Too late Michael realized he ought to have clamped a hand over his son's mouth the instant the lady's name came out of it. The room had gone strangely quiet. Every Bedwyn sibling was present except the Duke of Bewcastle. So were Lady Alleyne Bedwyn, the two men who were married to the Bedwyn sisters, the Reverend Charles Lofter, the Marquess of Attingsborough, and two other guests. All of them had just been treated to the announcement that Miss Thompson would have him if he wanted her.

"Robert, my lad," he said, "whatever have you been up to? And do I detect the devious mind of your sister behind it?"

"Georgie did not go, Papa," his son told him earnestly. "She could not. She had promised. So I went. And Miss Thompson said—"

"Right," Michael said briskly in the hearing of an audience whose members did not even pretend not to be avidly listening. "We had better find a private room somewhere to discuss this. About five minutes too late, I might add."

He did not look about him as he took Robert's hand in his and strode for the door. He did not even look to see whose hand came down on his shoulder and squeezed it sympathetically as they left the room. Good God. Really. Good God! If there were only a deep, dark hole available just beyond the billiard room, he would gladly jump into it and curl up there and never come out.

But...

She would have him?

Had she really said that? Had she meant it?

Really?

* * * * *

Eleanor spent an hour alone in her room in an attempt to compose herself and then went to her mother's sitting room, where she also found Hazel and Claudia and Eve, Lady Aidan Bedwyn. She stayed after everyone else had left and persuaded her mother to have luncheon brought up. If she could have thought of a good enough excuse—a crashing migraine headache? A touch of smallpox?—she would have stayed there all afternoon and evening and all of tomorrow. But alas, she had duties to perform. She had agreed to help organize the children's races.

Perhaps Robert had not said anything to his father. He knew, after all, that both he and his sister would be in trouble if the Earl of Staunton found out. But oh, dear, she had never felt more mortified in her life. What if Robert *had* told? It did not bear thinking of.

She left her room after dressing for the afternoon party and marched downstairs and outdoors with an almost martial stride. She was met with the reassuring sight of a number of house guests and neighbors invited for the occasion and hordes of exuberant, dashing, shrieking children. There was no sign of the Earl of Staunton or either of his children. And if it seemed that some of the house guests were looking at her with knowing smirks, then of course it was her imagination.

She continued her march to the lake and the area marked out for the races. The former Lady Morgan Bedwyn, now the Countess of Rosthorn, was some distance away, setting up for the archery contest. Her husband and Charles, Eleanor's brother-in-law, were organizing a skipping rope contest. Rannulf Bedwyn and his brother Alleyne were checking the boats, in which they would be giving rides. Eleanor's mother and Hazel were in the refreshment booth though a full-scale picnic tea would be served on the west lawn later. Judith, Lady Rannulf Bedwyn, was in the dress-up circle, where there were piles of old clothes and hats and fans and shoes and wigs culled from the attics so that the children could dress up to act out the stories she would tell. Freyja, Marchioness of Hallmere, was in charge of the rolling and tumbling races down the hill. A swimming area had been staked out at the lake and was to be supervised by

Joshua, the Marquess of Hallmere. Christine would play games with the infants whenever she could find a spare moment. Aidan Bedwyn was offering fencing lessons with wooden swords in a roped-off area under the trees. Rachel, Lady Alleyne Bedwyn, was organizing a stand of bright trinkets and confections, which could be purchased with one of the five tokens issued to each child at the start.

Eleanor was soon busy with Eve, Lady Aidan Bedwyn, organizing children into age groups, helping them wriggle into sacks for the sack race and tie them securely about their waists, making sure everyone stayed behind the starting line until the signal to begin was given. She picked up the smaller children when they toppled over and set them on their way again. She was soon flushed and laughing and forgot the horrible embarrassment of the morning. Until, that was, Georgette arrived to run the three-legged race for the over-tens with Lizzie, and their fathers came along behind them to watch.

"Oh, goodness," Eve said, "are you going to run the race, Lizzie? How splendidly brave of you."

"She is going to run it with me," Georgette said. "We will be close together— we have to be, don't we?—and will have our arms about each other's waist. We will need only one pair of eyes. We have been practicing."

"It is the rest of the runners who are splendidly brave," the Marquess of Attingsborough remarked, "to run against Lizzie and Georgette."

Eleanor helped all five teams bind their legs together. Georgette and Lizzie were giggling. Lizzie's dog was sitting alertly beside the marquess, panting, his eyes fixed upon his mistress. And then Eleanor straightened up and moved out of the way so that the race could begin—and her eyes met the Earl of Staunton's. He did not smile. Neither did she.

He *knew*, she thought.

Becky, Eve's daughter, and her brother Davy won the race with ease, not having stumbled or fallen even once. Lizzie and Georgette were last by a mile— or what would have been a mile if the track had been that long. They weaved about, fell, picked themselves up, weaved about again, fell again, and so on until they finally stumbled across the finish line and collapsed, giggling and clinging together while the other racers and all the adults in the vicinity applauded and even cheered.

"I don't think," Georgette said as she unbound their legs, "we won a prize, Lizzie." And they were off on an another paroxysm of snorting laughter.

"That was the last of the set of five races," Eve said. "It is time to call Wulfric to present the prizes."

Eleanor busied herself picking up and folding the cloths that had been used to bind legs, but she looked up when the Earl of Staunton spoke to her.

"I am so sorry," he said quietly. "You must have been horribly embarrassed."

"I was honored," she said, not pretending to misunderstand him, "to discover that that two young children who met me only briefly at a country inn thought they saw their ideal of a new mother in me. I am touched that even after almost two weeks here they remain attached to me. Your children's affection, so freely given, is like a precious gift that I will cherish in memory for a long time to come. You must not be embarrassed on my behalf, Lord Staunton, or on your own. I have no expectation of actually being their mother. I have a full life of my own that I enjoy."

"I know," he said. "Thank you for being so gracious. I have understood from your…manner during the past few days that you do not wish to encourage me to refine too much upon what happened during our walk together. You need have no fear that a pair of young matchmakers will harass you further or goad me into doing so. Ah, here comes Bewcastle."

Wulfric was indeed approaching, Lord Arthur Bedwyn, the younger of his sons and Eleanor's nephew, astride his shoulders and clinging to the underside of his chin with two plump little hands.

"Every participant in the races receives something, I gather?" the earl asked.

"But of course," she said. "There are no losers at this children's party. It is not like real life, thank goodness."

He moved away to join the Marquess of Attingsborough and their daughters, who were still in giggling high spirits, their arms still about each other's waist.

He had understood *from her manner*?

He would not be goaded into harassing her?

Was he merely being kind, implying that *she* was the one who wanted nothing to do with *him* when really it was the other way around? Or had he really misunderstood? She had certainly tried to behave with dignity during the past few days. She had not wanted him to feel—heaven forbid—that his kiss had inspired her with false hope. She had not wanted him to feel trapped. Had she at the same time given the impression that she did not *want* any further attentions?

Oh, how complicated life could be! She was too old for this.

He went away after Wulfric had presented the prizes, without looking again at her. He had said his piece, it seemed, and now it was over.

"The egg and spoon race next," Eve said. "This should be fun."

She was looking at Eleanor with…curiosity? Sympathy? Eleanor hoped fervently she was imagining things.

* * * * *

The great hall was a magnificent setting for the banquet. The orchestra that had been hired for the ball later provided soft music from the minstrel gallery— until a single bugle played a fanfare while everyone looked upward in surprise and delight and Wulfric looked with steady silver gaze along the length of the great oak table to where Christine was smiling sunnily back at him. He even raised his quizzing glass to his eye, but, quite uncowed, she smiled even more dazzlingly. The fanfare was the signal for Lord Aidan Bedwyn to rise to begin the speeches and make the first toasts to his elder brother.

The ballroom looked just as magnificent when they arrived there later. Eleanor took a seat beside her mother—she rarely danced at assemblies or balls. She was not even wearing an elaborate ballgown. Her light blue silk had done duty for several years and would do for one or two more. She was quite happy to watch the new arrivals as they moved along the receiving line. She recognized a number of the neighbors from other visits over the last five years. The Earl and Countess of Redfield had come from Alvesley Park with their sons Kit, Viscount Ravensberg, and Mr. Sydnam Butler and their wives. Mr. Butler's wife, Anne, had taught at the school in Bath for a few years when Claudia still owned it.

The ballroom was soon crowded. Miss Everly, dressed gorgeously in a shimmering pink gown, her mother in royal blue with an elaborate turban and towering hair plumes hovering at her side, had a small court of gentlemen about her. It did not, at least at the moment, include the Earl of Staunton. He, looking gloriously handsome in black evening clothes with crisp white linen, was chatting with Anne and Claudia and the Earl of Redfield.

His children, hand in hand, had knocked on the door of Eleanor's room after the children's party was over. They had both looked pale and stricken, and Georgette had rattled off an uncharacteristically brief apology for having bothered her and embarrassed her. Eleanor had stooped down and gathered them both into her arms and held them tightly.

"Oh, no," she had said. "No, no, no. Please do not apologize. I have felt so very honored to be liked by you, to have been singled out for your affections. Please do not be sorry. I love you both very dearly."

"But you will not be our mama?" Robert had whispered, clinging to her sleeve.

"She can't be, Robbie," Georgette had said through the tears that were welling into her eyes and trickling down her cheeks. "Not unless she marries Papa. Don't you love Papa, Miss Thompson?"

"Georgie," Robert had said, still whispering, "Papa said we were to say sorry and then leave."

"But don't you?" Georgette had wailed.

"I have a deep regard for him," Eleanor had said. "He is a wonderful father, is he not? And he is a very likable person."

"And he has a regard for you too," Georgette had said, pulling back from Eleanor's embrace. "He said so. Miss Thompson, why are adults so *stupid*? Why do they not say what they mean? And what they *feel*? Come on, Robbie, or we will be in trouble again."

"We were not in *trouble*, Georgie," he had said, taking her hand and turning away with her. "Papa did kiss us and tell us he understood, and he didn't *tell* us to come and say sorry. He only asked us if we thought perhaps we ought."

Eleanor shook her head slightly now and moved it closer to her mother to hear what she was saying.

A ball usually opened with a quadrille or a cheerful country dance. This ball, very unusually, was to open with a waltz. It had been Christine's idea. She and Wulfric were to dance the first part of the set alone together, and then everyone else would be invited to join in the other two parts. Wulfric had agreed after giving her a hard look.

"On the assumption, I suppose, my love," he had said, "that this may be my last chance to perform to an audience. By my forty-first birthday I may have become too arthritic to dance at all. Not to mention gout."

Eleanor stood to watch them dance. They always did it so well. Christine followed his lead as though she floated in his arms, her head tipped back, her eyes on his face, her smile soft and radiant as though she had only that moment fallen in love with him for the first time. And Wulfric waltzed very correctly but also with a certain flair that could not be described in words. And he looked back into his wife's face with his customary austere, even cold expression—yet with adoration somehow beaming from him too. Oh, it was impossible to put into words, even inside her own head. And it was equally impossible not to feel envy.

I have understood from your manner during the past week that you do not wish to encourage me to refine too much upon what happened during our walk together.

Eleanor sighed inwardly as the music drew to a close, and resumed her seat beside her mother while everyone applauded and other couples took their places on the floor for the second waltz of the set. If Gregory had lived, would they still be deeply in love all this time later? Would there—

"Miss Thompson." The Earl of Staunton was bowing to her and smiling at her mother. "Would you do me the honor of waltzing with me?"

Oh. She had not seen him approach. *Oh.* She stopped herself only just in time from folding her hands quietly in her lap and informing him that she did not dance. Good heavens, she might even have added that she was too *old* to dance. She was aware of her mother beside her, beaming from one to the other of them.

"Thank you," Eleanor said and got to her feet without smiling. She set her hand on his sleeve. She hoped—oh, dear, she hoped he had not felt obliged to ask her. But she shook her head slightly—*I have understood from your manner...* She looked up at him as they took their places on the floor, and set one hand on his shoulder as one of his came to rest behind her waist and his other clasped her free hand. And she smiled. She was not sure it was not a grimace. Her facial muscles felt tight.

"I understand," he said softly just before the music began, "that you have a deep regard for me just as I have for you, Miss Thompson. I also understand that adults are *stupid*—with emphasis, if you please. And since you and I are both adults, then I daresay we are also stupid."

The music began.

Eleanor knew the steps. She had waltzed on occasion. She had always been a little disappointed, for it was such a potentially romantic dance, and she had seen it done as it ought to be. She had seen it just a short while ago with her sister and brother-in-law, still obviously very deeply in love with each other even after five years of marriage and three children. She performed the steps now. So did he. He knew them well and danced with confidence. It was easy to follow his lead. After the first minute or so she relaxed despite the fact that his words—or rather Georgette's—were still whirling about in her head.

And suddenly it was no longer a mechanical exercise. Suddenly they were dancing and twirling and she was acutely aware of him—of the feel of his hands and the heat of his body and the solid firmness of his presence and the smell of his cologne—and of their surroundings too: the wheeling lights from the chandeliers, the smell of flowers and candles and perfumes, the kaleidoscope of colors as ladies in bright gowns twirled and flowers spilled over the sides of pots. Suddenly waltzing was the loveliest thing she had ever done, and she would never forget. Oh, she would never forget it—or him. And she would not remember with sadness. She would remember with gratitude that she had met him at all and spent brief moments of time with him. She might have gone through the rest of her life without even that much of a new dream.

She was smiling up into his face, she realized suddenly, and he was smiling back. Had her awareness only expanded beyond him, she might have noticed that a great deal of curious attention was upon the two of them, at least among the house guests, though most of them were also waltzing. But she was unaware and so she was unselfconscious.

"What manner?" she asked him when the music stopped. "What has my manner been like?"

"Forbidding," he said, but he was still smiling. "Warning me to keep my distance."

"I did not want you to think," she said, "that I was...well, *pursuing* you."

"And I did not want you to think," he said, "that I was in relentless pursuit of a mother for my children without any regard for you as a person. And without regard for your chosen way of life."

"My chosen way of life," she said. "I am selling my school. I have not been as happy since I purchased it as I was when I was simply a teacher. I do not know what I will do once it is sold. I will doubtless think of...something. But what of Miss Everly?"

"I made it clear to her and her mama before you and I went walking that afternoon," he said, "that there was no courtship between us and never really had been except in their imagination. It was my title and fortune that were the attraction, I have no doubt. Lady Connaught is determined that her daughter will make an advantageous marriage. I wish Miss Everly well, but she would not do as my wife, you know. And she certainly would not do as the mother of my children, both present and future."

Eleanor bit her lip and gazed back at him.

"Sometimes children possess a great deal of wisdom," he said. "I believe I have been stupid, Miss Thompson. And dare I hope, unmannerly as it seems, that you have been too?"

She released her lip. "Oh, I have," she said.

The third waltz of the set began. And if there was such a thing as magic, then someone must have waved a star-studded wand about their heads and created a world of music and dance and wonderment that enclosed them and became all their own. If only it could last forever.

He stood and gazed at her when it was over, making no move to return her to her mother's side. "I do not know what the next set is to be," he said, "or the one after that. I have absolutely no desire whatsoever to dance them, however. Do you?"

She shook her head.

"Come." He offered his arm and led her toward the open French windows and out onto the wide stone balcony beyond the ballroom. It was still deserted this early in the evening. "Miss Thompson—may I call you Eleanor?"

"Yes," she said, "Michael." Her heart was pounding so hard she felt breathless.

"Eleanor," he said, "I come encumbered with two children."

"Encumbered?" she said. "What a strange word."

"It is surely a thankless task to take on someone else's children," he said.

"Michael," she said, and she felt quite dizzy as she clung more tightly to his arm, "are you asking me to take them on?"

"The trouble is," he said, "that they have chosen you and have been embarrassingly public about it. Did you know that Robert announced your willingness to have me in a crowded billiard room this morning?"

Oh, dear. Oh, no!

"So you feel honor bound to offer for me?" she said

He uttered a muffled oath. "I would not have believed," he said, "that I could be so gauche, or so *stupid,* to use my daughter's word, as I have been recently. I am offering for you, Eleanor, because I believe we can be happy together even though we do not have a lengthy acquaintance. And because, at the advanced age of forty, I have fallen in love. Will you marry me?"

They were standing at the top of the steps leading down to the moonlit garden. They were still alone on the balcony.

"Oh," she said, "I cannot think of anything I would rather do. I love your children and delight in the prospect of being a mama to them. But I could not marry you just for their sakes. I do love you, Michael. It is absurd. The world would call it so anyway. We have known each other for such a short while, and for years past I have never thought to love again. But I do. I have dreamed a new dream in the last couple of weeks and it is already coming true. How well blessed I am. Yes, I will marry you."

There were people gathered close to the doorway behind them, talking and laughing. They might at any moment decide to step outside into the cooler air.

"It is not even cold out here, is it?" he said. "Or dark. Can I persuade you to stroll to the lake with me."

Oh. It would be very improper. But the thought gave her a smile. She was *thirty-nine* years old.

"What a lovely idea," she said.

He led her down the steps and around to the front of the house. As they passed in front of the fountain he released her arm and took her hand instead, lacing their fingers.

She laughed. "I feel like a girl again."

"Please do not." In the moonlight she could see that his eyes were smiling. "I am not interested in girls, Eleanor."

"Only in women?" she asked.

"Not even in women," he said. "In *one* woman. In you."

If this was a dream, she hoped she would not wake up soon. Or ever.

They stood for a while on the bank of the lake, looking out over the water. A band of moonlight beamed across it, showing the surface to be like glass. There was not a breath of wind. He let go of her hand and circled her waist with his arm. She set her own about his and rested the side of her head on his shoulder. Ah, she had not believed this could or would happen to her ever again. He turned his head and kissed her warmly on the lips.

"Eleanor," he asked, his mouth still almost brushing hers, "are you a virgin?"

Oh.

"No," she said, lifting her head. "He was going away to war, you must understand. We were both aware that he might never return. We were young and very much in love. And rash."

"You need not justify yourself," he said. "Will you come with me to that clearing among the trees where we kissed a few days ago?"

She drew a slow and audible breath.

"But only if you wish," he added.

"Oh," she said with a sigh, "I do indeed wish, Michael."

They walked there, their arms still about each other, and he shrugged out of his evening coat and spread it on the grass. She could not even remember those other times with Gregory—it had happened twice. But she did not want to remember. That was then and with the love of her youth. This was now with the love of her heart.

He loved her slowly and thoroughly after they had lain down together, his mouth and his hands caressing her through her clothing and beneath it while she touched him and felt all the warm, firm splendor of his man's body and all the wonder of knowing that they would spend the rest of their lives together. He did not unclothe her, only lifted her gown and removed essential items before unbuttoning the flap of his evening breeches and freeing himself. He came over onto her, cushioning her with his hands against the hardness of the ground, and when he entered her, he did so firmly but slowly, giving her time to adjust to the shock of the intimacy.

"You are so beautiful," he murmured against her mouth, And while she smiled at the extravagance of the word, she believed it too. She was neither pretty nor young, but at the moment she knew herself to be beautiful, for she was both lovable and loved and there was no better feeling in the world. Especially when she returned that love unconditionally and for all time. It did not matter that they had known each other for only a couple of weeks. It just did not matter.

He was a wonderful, skilled, patient lover. He took his time and gave her time while pleasure built to something that was almost painful and then burst into something beyond pain or pleasure while she felt him still and deep and hot in her and she shuddered into a relaxation more complete than any she had ever known.

"Ah, my love." His voice was deep against her ear.

"Mmm." She smiled.

They lay side by side, gazing up at moon and stars, dozing a little. An owl was hooting some distance away. There was the faint sound of music from the direction of the house. There was the soft lapping of water against the bank. Her fingers were laced with his again. The fingers of her other hand briefly touched the betrothal ring beneath the bodice of her gown, and she smiled a sad and final farewell to an old and precious love. Tonight she would remove the chain from about her neck. Tonight there was a new love, a new dream.

"It is going to have to be soon," he said, turning his face toward hers.

"Is it?" She had not even disentangled herself from her school yet. Reality was beginning to intrude.

"Georgette and Robert are going to be *very* impatient when they know we are betrothed," he said. "Not to mention ecstatic. And I might just have impregnated you, Eleanor. No, do not protest, as I suspect you are about to do, that you are too old. I would wager you are not. Most important of all, I do not want to wait and neither, I hope, do you. We may have the banns read here, if you insist, and wait a month. Or I will fetch a special license and we will marry within a week and you will come home with us. We will deal with your school together, or you may deal with it alone. But as a married lady, Eleanor. Tell me you choose the special license."

"Within a week?" She gazed into his face though it was in shadow.

"I know it seems an eternity," he said.

She laughed. "Are you always so impulsive?" she asked.

"No." She saw the flash of his teeth before he closed the distance between them and kissed her again. "Say yes."

"Yes," she said.

"We will tell your mother and sisters and the children in the morning before I dash away in pursuit of a license," he said. "Georgette may not stop talking until I return. I give you fair warning and apologize in advance."

"And I give you fair warning," she said, "that I will not stop listening to her and to Robert for a lifetime. Or loving them. I apologize in advance."

He slid his arm beneath her neck and turned her against him. "But tonight," he said, "I am selfishly delighted to have our happiness all to ourselves. I do love you, Eleanor. I would marry you twenty times over even if I had no children who needed you and schemed shamefully to get you."

"But once will be quite sufficient," she told him.

The moonlight had caught his face, and she could see the kindness, the happiness in his eyes and the curve of a smile on his lips. She gave him back the same look.

They were dreaming the same dream, she thought. Except that it was not a night dream. Rather, it was a life dream and would carry them through all the highs and lows of marriage and of life itself. She had never been more sure of anything in her life.

"I must get you back to the ballroom," he said.

"Yes."

But he kissed her again, and it was a full half hour later before an avidly curious gathering of relatives and friends were able to see that yes, indeed, there *was* a romance between those two.

Probably more than a romance.

CHAPTER 8

Five days after the birthday celebrations for Wulfric, Duke of Bewcastle, the grand medieval hall was again being set up for yet another banquet. This time the occasion was the wedding of the duchess's sister, Miss Eleanor Thompson, to Michael, Earl of Staunton. But the lavish breakfast would not be served until after the nuptial service in the village church and that would not begin for another half hour.

Wulfric awaited the appearance of his sister-in-law. Christine and Hazel and their mother had told him a few minutes ago that she was ready and would be down almost immediately. All three of them had looked a bit dewy-eyed as he had escorted them outside and handed them into the carriage that awaited them. They were the last of the guests to leave. The others had gone earlier, adults and children alike—all the children, even the babies, including Lady Caroline Bedwyn, Wulfric's own three-month old.

Eleanor had asked him if he would give her away at her wedding. The problem of which of her two favorite brothers-in-law she should ask was made considerably easier for her, she had explained, her eyes twinkling, after Charles had agreed to Michael's request that he co-celebrate the nuptials with the local rector.

Staunton had asked Wulfric rather late on the evening of the birthday ball to make the betrothal announcement. He had also asked, before the announcement was made, if the wedding could be solemnized here in the village church just as soon as he could fetch a special license and talk to the rector. The whole thing had been remarkably easy to arrange. The rector and his wife had been at the ball, and he had agreed with a hearty rubbing of his hands to officiate at the happy event at a moment's notice, provided the groom arrived at the church with the proper documentation and preferably with a ring for the bride's finger. He had been equally delighted to include the Reverend Charles Lofter in the service. And as for the rest—well, Christine was Wulfric's duchess. No more needed to be said.

Staunton had left Lindsey Hall at the crack of dawn the morning after the ball, having first woken his children to explain the situation to them. He had returned yesterday, early in the afternoon, and the assembled Bedwyns and their spouses and the Lofters and the other house guests, all of whom had stayed with the obvious exceptions of Lady Connaught and Miss Everly, had been informed that today would be the day.

When Eleanor stepped into the great hall and glanced about her at all the bustle of preparation and then looked at Wulfric, it occurred to him that she looked at least five years younger than she had the first time he had seen her. It was not that she was dressed like a blushing bride fresh out of the schoolroom. Indeed, he would be very surprised if he had not seen that blue dress on her more than once before. And her hair was not dressed any more elaborately than usual. The brim of her bonnet had been newly trimmed with what looked like fresh flowers, it was true, and she was carrying a small posy of matching flowers in one gloved hand. But it was none of those things that had stripped years from her age.

It was—indeed it had to be because Christine had told Wulfric so a number of times during the past few days, and he would not have dreamed of arguing with his duchess upon a matter in which she was a self-styled expert—it was, in fact, love.

And though he looked upon his sister-in-law with his customary austere expression and with silver eyes that very rarely hinted at any warmth he might be feeling within, nevertheless Wulfric regarded her with affection and approval. A bride ought to be in love with her bridegroom, just as a groom ought to be in love with his bride.

He knew it from personal experience.

"You are looking very fetching, Eleanor," he told her, offering his arm.

"You are kind, Wulfric," she said. "My mirror tells me I will do—provided, that is, we proceed to the church without any delay before my flowers wilt."

It was the sort of reply he might have expected of her—though she proceeded to spoil the effect almost immediately. "Oh," she said, taking his arm and clutching it, "is it natural to feel so very nervous?"

He led her from the house to the waiting carriage. "I do believe," he said, "it would be quite *unnatural* not to."

* * * * *

The village church was quite respectably full though only two members of the congregation belonged to Michael. They were enough. Eleanor had expressed concern about it and had offered to be patient and wait until all his relatives and any particular friends of his could be summoned. He had been unwilling to wait any longer, however. He had fallen unexpectedly in love and he did not want to delay any part of his future. His children had also fallen in love, and making them wait might have provoked a near mutiny.

Georgette was out of sight at the back of the church with the Duchess of Bewcastle and Mrs. Lofter. She was wearing a new pink party dress he had bought hurriedly in London, hoping it would fit her and be something of which she approved. He had been fortunate on both counts. She had a task to perform today. She was to walk down the nave of the church behind Eleanor, and she was to stand beside her during the service to hold her flowers and her gloves.

Robert, dressed in his new clothes, was seated against Michael's side in the front pew. Mrs. Harris had plastered his hair to his head before they left the house, but by now it was its usual blond fuzz—rather like a halo. Robert too had a task to perform. Michael had dispensed with the offices of a best man. His son would stand beside him and hand him the ring when the time came. Strangely, it had not seemed to occur to Robert to be nervous about it or to fear that he might drop the ring.

"When will Mama come?" he asked in a loud whisper. "Will I be able to call her that soon, Papa?"

"Very soon," Michael said as a slight bustle at the back of the church heralded the appearance of Lofter and the rector, who gave the signal for the congregation to stand. The organ struck a chord.

And she came toward him along the nave, her arm drawn through Bewcastle's. And Michael, far from feeling nervous, felt a rush of gladness that a certain thunderstorm had stranded them together at the same small inn three weeks ago—was it really no longer ago than that?—and that Georgette had invited herself to take tea with Eleanor in the dining room. It was true that they would have met anyway and spent two weeks at the same house party here, but would they have made the connection if it had not been for that storm? Would the children have made the connection?

She looked familiar, beautiful, dearly beloved, and he felt himself smiling warmly at her even as she smiled at him.

Robert, he could feel, was clutching one of the tails of his coat. Georgette was peeping around Eleanor and beaming at him.

They turned together to face the clergymen. And so it began—their new life together, a new dream to replace the old. No, not to replace it—to *add* to it. For they had both sincerely loved before and they had both suffered loss. They had both mourned and would forever remember. But now, today, there was another dream to promise present and future happiness.

* * * * *

Nervousness fled as soon as Eleanor stepped inside the church and saw Christine and Hazel awaiting her there and Georgette, her face alight with excitement. She was actually jumping up and down on the spot, her pink froth of a dress notwithstanding.

"I am going to hold your gloves and your flowers," she said, "and I am not going to crease the gloves or crush the flowers or drop anything, and I am—"

Eleanor cupped her face with her hands and kissed her.

"I know, sweetheart," she said, recognizing terrible nervousness when she saw it. "But it would not matter dreadfully even if you did do any of those unspeakable things."

And then, as she made her way along the nave on Wulfric's very sturdy arm and saw Michael waiting for her, looking immaculate and elegant in black and snowy white, it was the happiness and the kindness in his face that struck her more than anything else. She had never in her life done anything more right than what she was doing now, she thought. She had never been happier—and she was not even married yet.

Robert, clutching one of the tails of his father's coat, was peering around his leg, his eyes wide, his hair wild and adorable.

And then the nuptial service began, and while Eleanor was still trying to concentrate upon and savor every single moment of it, it was over and Charles, beaming kindly from one to the other of them, was informing them that they were man and wife. Eleanor thought she might well burst with happiness.

"Papa," a whispered voice asked, "may we call her Mama now?"

The congregation laughed—and applauded. It was an astonishing moment. Applause inside a church at the conclusion of a solemn ceremony? Michael bent down and scooped Robert up with one arm, and Eleanor wrapped an arm about the shoulders of Georgette, who had moved up close beside her.

"You may," she said softly, looking from one to the other of the children as Michael set his free hand on his daughter's head. "Oh, yes, indeed you may."

And they went off together as a family with their chosen witnesses—Wulfric and the Earl of Ravensberg—to sign the register. And then they were back inside the church and walking up the nave, smiling from side to side at their guests gathered there, and Eleanor knew that this was without any doubt the happiest day of her life, as a woman's wedding day ought to be.

"Oh—trouble," she said without any great surprise as they emerged from the church into bright sunshine and looked along the winding path of the churchyard to the gates and the gathering of numerous villagers beyond them. But within the gates and beneath the shade of the great elm tree that hung over the path, waited the Bedwyn men and the spouses of the Bedwyn women and a few of the other male house guests and some of the older children too. They all clutched fistfuls of flower petals, which were soon raining down upon the bride and groom and their children.

"It would be mean-spirited," Michael said, "to saunter along the path as though we did not mind or even enjoyed the experience, would it not? Shriek, Georgette. Roar, Robert. Take my hand, Eleanor, and prepare to dash."

They broke into a run, laughing helplessly as they went while Georgette obligingly screamed and Robert giggled and clung to his father's neck.

The ordeal was not over when they were through the gates, of course. The open barouche, decorated festively with flowers and ribbons, also bore all the old, metallic paraphernalia that Eleanor remembered from other people's weddings. As soon as the carriage was in motion, the noise would be deafening. Now the noise was only joyful. There was the sound of people calling out and laughing, and the church bells were pealing out the news of a new marriage.

They settled in the barouche as the congregation—or what was left of it—began to spill from the church. They were all on the same seat, Robert on Eleanor's lap, Georgette squeezed between her and her father.

"Lean back for a moment, Georgie," Michael said, spreading one arm over the back of the seat as the barouche rocked into motion. And he leaned across his daughter and kissed Eleanor on the lips and smiled into her eyes.

The bells pealed joyously, the guests and the villagers cheered the kiss—and an unholy din blocked it all out. His smile turned to laughter as Eleanor laughed back at him and Robert clapped his hands over his ears and Georgette threw back her head and whooped at the summer sky.

THE END

Dear Reader,

May, 2016, will see the publication of **Only Beloved**, the seventh and final book of the Survivors' Club series. Five men and one woman, variously wounded in the Napoleonic Wars, spent three years together at Penderris Hall in Cornwall, home of the Duke of Stanbrook, recovering from their wounds and forging a lifelong friendship and support group with the duke and one another. During the following years, each adjusted to a life that had changed beyond recognition, and each found love and happiness. Now, in the seventh book it is George, Duke of Stanbrook's turn. He gave of his home, his time, and his very self for the others, but now he is alone and lonely and restless. He did not fight in the wars, but his only son did and lost his life—and his wife committed suicide a few months later. George is not sure life can offer him any future happiness, but he surely deserves his happily ever after.

Dora Debbins first appeared in **Only Enchanting**, Book 4 of the series, as the heroine's older sister. Dora had given up her youth and her own chance for marriage and happiness in order to bring up her young sister after their mother ran away from home with a lover. When Agnes married one of the Survivors, Dora was left to her quiet, solitary life as a music teacher in a small village—and to her memories of a few glorious days when she met and fell in love with the Duke of Stanbrook. She does not expect ever to see him again. But she too surely deserves some happiness of her own.

George does remember Dora, and he makes a sudden, impulsive decision to travel into the country to see her again. Below is a brief glimpse of what happens when he arrives there. Dora has just returned home to her little cottage after a day of teaching private pupils, and she is weary. All she wants to do is sit alone in her sitting room and enjoy a cup of tea.

Enjoy the excerpt—and the book.

Mary Balogh
www.marybalogh.com
www.facebook.com/AuthorMaryBalogh

Only Beloved

CHAPTER 1

She picked up her cup and sipped her tea. But it had grown tepid and she pulled a face. It was entirely her own fault, of course. But she hated tea that was not piping hot.

And then a knock sounded on the outer door. Dora sighed. She was just too weary to deal with any chance caller. Her last pupil for the day had been fourteen-year-old Miranda Corley, who was as reluctant to play the pianoforte as Dora was to teach her. She was utterly devoid of musical talent, poor girl, though her parents were convinced she was a prodigy. Those lessons were always a trial to them both.

Perhaps Mrs. Henry would deal with whoever was standing on her doorstep. Her housekeeper knew how tired she always was after a full day of giving lessons and guarded her privacy a bit like a mother hen. But this was not to be one of those occasions, it seemed. There was a tap on the sitting room door, and Mrs. Henry opened it and stood there for a moment, her eyes as wide as twin saucers.

"It is for you, Miss Debbins," she said before stepping to one side.

And, as though her memories of last year had summoned him right to her sitting room, in walked the Duke of Stanbrook.

He stopped just inside the door while Mrs. Henry closed it behind him.

"Miss Debbins," He bowed to her. "I trust I have not called at an inconvenient time?"

Any comfort Dora had drawn during those few days last year from a realization that he was kindly and approachable and really quite human fled without a trace, and she was every bit as smitten by awe as she had been when she met him for the first time in the drawing room at Middlebury Park. He was tall and distinguished looking, with dark hair silvered at the temples, and austere, chiseled features consisting of a straight nose, high cheekbones and rather thin lips. He bore himself with a stiff, forbidding air she did not remember from last year. He was the quintessential fashionable, aloof aristocrat from head to toe, and he seemed to fill Dora's sitting room and deprive it of most of the breathable air.

She realized suddenly that she was still sitting and staring at him all agape, like a thunderstruck idiot. He had spoken to her in the form of a question and was regarding her with raised eyebrows in expectation of an answer. She scrambled belatedly to her feet and curtsied. She tried to remember what she was wearing and whether her garments included a cap.

"Your Grace," she said. "No, not at all. I have given my last music lesson for the day and have been having my tea. The tea will be cold in the pot by now. Let me ask Mrs. Henry—"

But he had held up one elegant staying hand.

"Pray do not concern yourself," he said. "I have just finished taking refreshments with Vincent and Sophia."

With Viscount and Lady Darleigh.

"I was at Middlebury Park earlier today," she said, "giving Lady Darleigh a pianoforte lesson since she missed her regular one while she was in London for Lady Barclay's wedding. She did not say anything about your having come back with them. Not that she was obliged to do so, of course." Her cheeks grew hot. "It was none of my business."

"I arrived an hour ago," he told her, "unexpected but not quite uninvited. Every time I see Vincent and his lady, they urge me to visit any time I wish. They always mean it just as they never expect that I will come. This time I did. I followed almost upon their heels from London, in fact, and, bless their hearts, I do believe they were happy to see me. Or not see in Vincent's case. Sometimes one almost forgets that he cannot literally see."

Dora's cheeks grew hotter. For how long had she been keeping him standing there by the door? Whatever would he think of her rustic manners?

"But will you not have a seat, Your Grace?" She indicated the chair across the hearth from her own. "Did you walk from Middlebury? It is a lovely day for air and exercise, though, is it not?"

He had arrived from London an hour ago? He had taken tea with Viscount and Lady Darleigh and had stepped out immediately after to come…here? Perhaps he brought a message from Agnes?

"I will not sit," he said. "This is not really a social call."

"Agnes—?" Her hand crept to her throat. His stiff, formal manner was suddenly explained. There was something wrong with Agnes. She had miscarried.

"Your sister appeared to be glowing with good health when I saw her a few days ago," he said. "I am sorry if my sudden appearance has alarmed you. I came to ask a question."

Dora clasped both hands at her waist and waited for him to continue. A day or two after she had played for the guests at Middlebury last year he had come to the cottage with a few of the others to thank her for playing and to express the hope that she would do so again before their visit came to an end. It had not happened. Was he going to ask now? For this evening, perhaps? Suddenly she forgot her weariness.

"I wondered, Miss Debbins," he said, "if you would do me the great honor of marrying me."

Duke of
My Dreams

GRACE BURROWES

To the odd ducks

CHAPTER 1

"I do not ask this boon of you lightly."

Elias, Duke of Sedgemere, strolled along, damned if he'd embarrass Hardcastle with any show of sentiment in the face of Hardcastle's wheedling. Hardcastle was, after all, Sedgemere's oldest and dearest friend too.

Also Sedgemere's only friend.

They took the air beside Hyde Park's Serpentine, ignoring the stares and whispers they attracted. While Sedgemere was a blond so pale as to draw the eye, Hardcastle was dark. They were both above average in height and brawn, though Mayfair boasted any number of large, well-dressed men, particularly as the fashionable hour approached.

They were dukes, however, and to be a duke was to be afflicted with public interest on every hand. To be an *unmarried* duke was to be cursed, for in every ballroom, at the reins of every cabriolet, holding every parasol, was a duchess-in-waiting.

Thus Sedgemere endured Hardcastle's importuning.

"You do not ask a boon," Sedgemere said, tipping his hat to a fellow walking an enormous brindle mastiff. "You demand half my summer, when summer is the best time of year to bide at Sedgemere House."

They had known each other since the casual brutality and near starvation that passed for a boy's indoctrination at Eton, and through the wenching and wagering that masqueraded as an Oxford education. Hardcastle, however, had never married, and thus knew not what horrors awaited him on the way to the altar.

Sedgemere knew, and he further knew that Hardcastle's days as a bachelor were numbered, if Hardcastle's estimable grandmama was dispatching him to summer house parties.

"If you do not come with me, Sedgemere, I will become a bad influence on my godson. I will teach the boy about cigars, brandy, fast women, and profligate gambling."

"The child is seven years old, Hardcastle, but feel free to corrupt him at your leisure, assuming he does not prove to be the worse influence on—good God, not these two again."

The Cheshire twins, blond, blue-eyed, smiling, and as relentless as an unmentionable disease, came twittering down the path, twirling matching parasols.

"Miss Cheshire, Miss Sharon," Hardcastle said, tipping his hat.

Sedgemere discreetly yanked on his friend's arm, though nothing would do but Hardcastle must exchange pleasantries as if these women weren't the social equivalent of Scylla and Charybdis.

"Ladies." Sedgemere bowed as well, for he was in public and the murder of a best friend was better undertaken in private.

"Your Graces! How fortunate that we should meet!" Miss Cheshire gushed. The elder by four minutes, as Sedgemere had been informed on at least a hundred occasions, she generally led the conversational charges. "I told Sharon this very morning that you could not possibly have left Town without calling upon us, and I see I was right, for here you both are!"

Exactly where Sedgemere did not want to be.

"We'll take our leave of—" Sedgemere began, just as Hardcastle winged an arm.

"A pleasant day for pleasant company," Hardcastle said.

Miss Cheshire latched on to Hardcastle like a Haymarket streetwalker clutched her last penny's worth of gin, and Miss Sharon appropriated Sedgemere's arm without him even offering.

"You weren't planning to call on us, were you?"

Miss Sharon posed exactly the sort of query a man who'd endured five years of matrimonial purgatory knew better than to answer. If Sedgemere admitted that he'd no intention of calling on anybody before departing London, the Cheshire chit would pout, tear up, and try to shame him into an apology-call. If he lied and protested that, of course he'd been planning on calling, she'd assign him a time and date, and be sure to have her bosom bows lying in ambush with her in her mama's parlor.

Abruptly, three weeks trudging about the hills of the Lake District loomed not as a penance owed a dear friend, but as a reprieve, even if it meant uprooting the boys.

"My plans are not yet entirely made," Sedgemere said. "Though Hardcastle and I will both be leaving Town shortly."

Miss Sharon was desolated to hear this, though everybody left the pestilential heat of a London summer if they could. She cooed and twittered and clung from one end of the Serpentine to the other, until Sedgemere was tempted to push her into the water simply to silence her.

"We bid you *adieu*," Hardcastle said, tipping his hat once more, fifty interminable, cooing, clutching yards later. "And we bid you farewell, for as Sedgemere says, the time has come for ruralizing. I'm sure we'll see both of you when we return to London."

Hardcastle was up to something, Sedgemere knew not what. Hardcastle was a civil fellow, though not even the Cheshire twins would accuse him of charm. Sedgemere liked that about him, liked that one man could be relied upon to be honest at all times, about all matters. Unfortunately, such guilelessness would make Hardcastle a lamb to slaughter among the house-party set.

Amid much simpering and parasol twirling, the Cheshire ladies minced back to Park Lane, there to lurk like trolls under a bridge until the next titled bachelor came along to enjoy the fresh air.

"Turn around now," Sedgemere said, taking Hardcastle by the arm and walking him back the way they'd come. "Before they start fluttering handkerchiefs as if the Navy were departing for Egypt. I suppose you leave me no choice but to accompany you on this infernal frolic to the Lakes."

"Because you are turning into a bore and a disgrace and must hide up north?" Hardcastle inquired pleasantly.

"Because there's safety in numbers, you dolt. Because if Miss Cheshire had sprung that question on you, about whether you intended to call, you would have answered her, and spent half of Tuesday in her mama's parlor, dodging debutante décolletages and tea trays."

Marriage imbued a man with instincts, or perhaps fatherhood did. Hardcastle was merely an uncle, but that privileged status meant he had his heir without having stuck the ducal foot in parson's mousetrap.

"I say, that is a handsome woman," Hardcastle muttered. Hardcastle did not notice women, but an octogenarian Puritan would have taken a closer look at the vision approaching on the path.

"Miss Anne Faraday," Sedgemere said, a comely specimen indeed. Tall, unfashionably curvaceous, unfashionably dark-haired, she was also one of few women whose company did not send Sedgemere into a foul humor. In fact, her approach occasioned something like relief.

"You're not dodging off into the rhododendrons," Hardcastle said, "and yet you seem to know her."

Would Miss Faraday acknowledge Sedgemere? She was well beyond her come out, and no respecter of dukes, single or otherwise.

"I don't know her well, but I like her very much," Sedgemere said. "She hates me, you see. Has no marital aspirations in my direction whatsoever. For that alone, she enjoys my most sincere esteem."

* * * * *

Effie was chattering about the great burden of having to pack up Anne's dresses in this heat, and about the dust of the road, and all the ghastly impositions on a lady's maid resulting from travel to the countryside at the end of the Season.

Anne half-listened, but mostly she was absorbed with the effort of *not* noticing. She did not notice the Cheshire twins, for example, all but cutting her in public. They literally could not afford to cut her. Neither could the Henderson heir, who merely touched his hat brim to her as if he couldn't recall that he'd seen her in Papa's formal parlor not three days ago. Mr. Willow Dorning, an earl's spare who was rumored to enjoy the company of dogs more than people, offered her a genuine, if shy, smile.

If Anne wanted freedom from Papa's sad eyes and long-suffering sighs, the price she paid was not noticing that, even in the genteel confines of Hyde Park, most of polite society was not very polite at all—to her.

"It's that dook," Effie muttered, "the ice dook, they call him."

"He's not icy, Effie. Sedgemere is simply full of his own consequence."

And why shouldn't he be? He was handsome in a rigid, frigid way, with white-gold hair that no breeze would dare ruffle. His features were an assemblage of patrician attributes—a nose well suited to being looked down, a mouth more full than expected, but no matter, for Anne had never seen that mouth smile. Sedgemere's eyes were a disturbingly pale blue, as if some Viking ancestor looked out of them, one having a grand sulk to be stranded so far from his frozen landscapes and turbulent seas.

"Your papa could buy and sell the consequence of any three dooks, miss, and well they know it."

"The problem in a nutshell," Anne murmured as Sedgemere's gaze lit on her.

He was in company with the Duke of Hardcastle, whom Anne had heard described as semi-eligible. Hardcastle had an heir, twelve estates, and a dragon for a grandmother. He was notably reserved, though Anne liked what she knew of him. He wasn't prone to staring at bosoms, for example.

Always a fine quality in a man.

Sedgemere was even wealthier than Hardcastle, had neither mama nor extant duchess, but was father to three boys. To Anne's dismay, His Grace of Sedgemere did not merely touch a gloved finger to his hat brim, he instead doffed his hat and bowed.

"Miss Faraday, hello."

She was so surprised, her curtseys lacked the proper deferential depth. "Your Graces, good day."

Then came the moment Anne dreaded most, when instead of not-noticing her, a scion of polite society *did* notice her, simply for the pleasure of brushing her aside. Sedgemere had yet to indulge in that particular sport with her, but he too, had visited in Papa's parlor more than once.

"Shall you walk with us for a moment?" Sedgemere asked. "I believe you know Hardcastle, or I'd perform the introductions."

A large ducal elbow aimed itself in Anne's direction. Such an elbow never came her way unless the duke in question owed Papa at least ten thousand pounds.

"Sedgemere's on his best behavior," Hardcastle said, taking Anne's other arm, "because if you tolerate his escort, then he'll not find other ladies plaguing him. The debutantes fancy Sedgemere violently this time of year."

The social Season was wrapping up, and too many families with daughters had endured the expense of a London Season without a marriage proposal to show for their efforts. Papa made fortunes off the social aspirations of the *beau monde*, while Anne—with no effort whatsoever—made enemies.

"The young ladies fancy unmarried dukes any time of year," Anne replied. Nonetheless, when Sedgemere tucked her hand onto his arm, she allowed it. This time tomorrow, she'd be well away from London, and the awful accusations resulting from a chance meeting in the park would never reach her ears.

The gossips would say that the presuming, unfortunate Anne Faraday was after a duke. No, that she was after two dukes.

Or perhaps, wicked creature that she was, she would pursue a royal duke next, for her father could afford even a royal husband for her.

"Will you spend the summer in Town, ma'am?" Hardcastle asked.

"Likely not, Your Grace. Papa's business means he will remain here, but he prefers that I spend some time in the shires, if possible."

"You always mention your father's business as early in a conversation as possible," Sedgemere said.

Anne could not decipher Sedgemere. His expression was as unreadable as a winter sky. If he'd been insulting her, the angle of his attack was subtle.

"I merely answered His Grace of Hardcastle's question. What of Your Graces? Will you soon leave for the country?"

Miss Helen Trimble and Lady Evette Hartley strolled past, and the consternation on their faces was almost worth the beating Anne's reputation would take once they were out of earshot. The gentlemen tipped their hats, the ladies dipped quick curtseys. Hardcastle was inveigled into accompanying the ladies to the gates of the park, and then—

Like a proud debutante poised in her newest finery at the top of the ballroom stairs, Sedgemere had come to a full stop.

"Your Grace?" Anne prompted, tugging on Sedgemere's arm.

"They did not acknowledge you. Those *women* did not so much as greet you. You might have been one of Mr. Dorning's mongrel dogs."

Well, no, because Mr. Dorning's canines were famously well-mannered, and thus endured much cooing and fawning from the ladies. Abruptly, Anne wished she could scurry off across the grass, and bedamned to manners, dukes, and young women who were terrified of growing old without a husband.

"The ladies often don't acknowledge me, Your Grace. I wish you would not remark it. The agreement we have is that they don't notice me, and I don't notice their rudeness. You will please neglect to mention this to my father."

As calculating as Papa was in business, he was a tender-hearted innocent when it came to ballroom warfare. In Papa's mind, his little girl—all nearly six feet of her—was simply too intelligent, pretty, sophisticated, and lovely for the friendship of the simpering twits and lisping viscounts.

"An agreement not to notice you?" Sedgemere snapped. "Who made such an agreement? Not that pair of dowdy poseurs. They couldn't agree on how to tie their bonnet ribbons."

The park was at its best as summer advanced, while all the rest of London became malodorous and stifling. The fashionable hour was about to begin, and thus the duke's behavior would soon attract notice.

"Your Grace will please refrain from making a scene," Anne said through gritted teeth. "I am the daughter of a man who holds the vowels of half the papas, uncles, and brothers of polite society. The ladies resent that, even if they aren't privy to the specifics."

Anne wasn't privy to the specifics either, thank heavens.

Sedgemere condescended to resume sauntering, leading Anne away from the Park Lane gates, deeper into the park's quiet greenery. She at first thought he was simply obliging her request, but a muscle leapt along his jaw.

"I'm sorry," Anne said. "If you owe Papa money, I assure you I'm not aware of it. He's most discreet, and I would never pry, and it's of no moment to me whether—"

"Hush," Sedgemere growled. "I'm trying to behave. One mustn't use foul language before a lady. Those women were ridiculous."

"They were polite to you," Anne said.

"Everybody is polite to a duke. It's nauseating."

"Everybody is rude to a banker's daughter. That's not exactly pleasant either, Your Grace."

The rudeness wasn't the worst of it, though. Worse than the cold stares, sneering smiles, and snide innuendos were the men. Certain titled bachelors saw Anne as a source of cash, which her father should be eager to turn over to them in exchange for allowing her to bear their titled heirs.

Which indelicate undertaking might kill her, of course.

Such men appraised her figure and her face as if she were a mare at Tatt's, a little long in the tooth, her bloodlines nondescript, though she was handsome enough for an afternoon ride.

"Everybody is rude to you?" Sedgemere asked.

Sedgemere carried disdain around with him like an expensive cape draped over his arm, visible at twenty paces, unlikely to be mislaid. His curiosity, as if

Anne's situation were a social experiment, and she responsible for reporting its results, disappointed her.

She hadn't thought she could be any more disappointed, not in a titled gentleman anyway.

"Must you make sport of my circumstances, Your Grace? Perhaps you'd care to take yourself off now. My maid will see me home."

He came to a leisurely halt and tucked his gloved hand over Anne's knuckles, so she could not free herself of him without drawing notice.

"You are sending me away," he said. "A duke of the realm, fifty-third in line for the throne, and you're sending me packing like a presuming, jug-eared footman who neglected to chew adequate quantities of parsley after overimbibing. Hardcastle will not believe this."

Incredulity was apparently in the air, for Anne could not believe what she beheld either. The Duke of Sedgemere, he of the icy eyes and frosty condescension, was regarding her with something approaching curiosity. Interest, at least, and not the sort of interest that involved her bosom.

"Perhaps you'd better toddle on, then," Anne said. "I'm sure there's a debutante—or twelve—who will expire of despair if she can't flaunt her wares at you before sundown."

"I'm dismissed out of hand, and now I'm to toddle. Dukes do not toddle, madam. Perhaps the heat is affecting your judgment." His tone would have frozen the Serpentine to a thickness of several inches.

Sedgemere, poor man, must owe Papa a very great deal of money.

"*Good day*, Your Grace. Have a pleasant summer."

Anne did not curtsey, because Sedgemere's scolding and sniffing had brought her unaccountably near tears. She was wealthy, a commoner, female, and unmarried. Her transgressions were beyond redemption, but why must Sedgemere blame her for circumstances she'd had no hand in creating?

Why must everybody?

Anne would have made a grand exit toward the Long Water, but some fool duke had trapped her hand in his.

"I must make allowances," he said, his grip on Anne's fingers snug. "You're not used to the undivided attention of so lofty a personage as I, and the day is rather warm. When next we meet, I assure you I will have the toddling well in hand. I enjoy a challenge, you see. You have a pleasant summer too, Miss Faraday, and my kindest regards to your dear papa."

Sedgemere's demeanor remained crushingly correct as he bowed with utmost graciousness over Anne's hand. When he tipped his hat to her, she could have sworn those chilly blue eyes had gained a hint of warmth.

He was laughing at her then, but half the polite world would have seen him bowing over Anne's hand, so she was at least a private joke.

"Thank you, Your Grace. Effie, come along. A lofty personage cannot be unnecessarily detained without serious consequences to the foolish woman who'd linger in his presence."

When Anne swept off at a brisk pace, the duke let her go, which was prudent of him. She was not above using her reticule as a weapon, and not even Sedgemere would have managed loftiness had Anne's copy of *The Mysteries of Udolpho* connected with the duke's… knees.

"The Quality is daft," Effie huffed at Anne's side. "Dafter by the year, miss, though he seemed nice enough, for a dook."

"Effie Carsdale! You were calling him icy not five minutes ago."

Sedgemere was cold, but not… not as easily dismissed as Anne had wanted him to be. He noticed where others ignored, he ignored what others dwelled upon—Anne's bosom, for example.

"Nice in an icy way," Effie clarified. "Been an age since anybody teased you, miss. Perhaps you've lost the habit of teasing back."

Anne's steps slowed. Ducks went paddling by on the mirror-flat water to the left. In the tall trees, birds flitted, and across the Serpentine, carriages tooled down Rotten Row. Another pretty day in the park, and yet…

"You think Sedgemere was *teasing* me?"

Effie was probably ten years Anne's senior, by no means old. She studied the trees overhead, she studied her toes. She was a bright woman, full of practical wisdom and pragmatism.

"I was teased by a duke and didn't even know it," Anne said, wishing she could run after Sedgemere and apologize. "I thought he was ridiculing me, Effie. They all ridicule me, while they take Papa's money to cover their inane bets."

And they were all polite to Sedgemere, which he apparently found as trying as insults.

"You'll have the last laugh, Miss Anne," Effie said. "Mark me, that dook will lead you out, come the Little Season, but thank goodness we'll soon be away from the wretched city. A few weeks breathing the fresh air, enjoying the lovely scenery up in the Lake District will put you to rights, see if it don't."

CHAPTER 2

Part of the reason Sedgemere had agreed to join Hardcastle at the Duke of Veramoor's "little gathering" was that Sedgemere House lay in Nottinghamshire, partway between London and the Lakes, and thus Sedgemere could dragoon his friend into visiting the Sedgemere family seat.

Hardcastle was nearly impossible to pry away from his ancestral pile in Kent, but he was godfather to Sedgemere's eldest, an imp of the devil named Alasdair.

"I've left instructions the boy's to use the courtesy title, having turned seven," Sedgemere said as he and Hardcastle moved their horses to the verge to make way for a passing coach. "The twins insist on thwarting my orders, of course, because it irritates their older brother."

A plume of dust hung in the morning air as the coach rattled by. The sun was so hot every sheep in the nearby pasture was panting, curled in the grass in the shade of a lone oak.

"Perhaps," Hardcastle replied, "the twins thwart your orders because they're barely six years old and have always known their brother by his name. My brother never referred to me by anything save my name when we were private."

Hardcastle was a good traveling companion, offering an argument to nearly every comment, observation, or casual aside Sedgemere tossed out. The miles went faster that way, and when traveling from London to Nottinghamshire, one endured many dusty, weary miles.

"You're nervous of this house party," Sedgemere said. "You needn't be. Simply follow the rules, Hardcastle, and you'll get some rest, catch a few fish, read a few poems. Veramoor is a duke first, a matchmaker second."

Or so Her Grace of Veramoor had assured Sedgemere, though one never entirely trusted a duchess with twelve happily married offspring. Thus Sedgemere had rules for surviving house parties: safety in numbers, never be alone in one's room without a chair wedged beneath the door, never over-imbibe, never show marked favor to any female, always ride out in company.

"You do recall the rules, Gerard?"

"Don't be tedious."

Sedgemere had used Hardcastle's Christian name advisedly, there being no one else left to extend him that kindness when he clearly missed his late brother. Hardcastle acknowledged Sedgemere's consideration by keeping his gaze on the road ahead as they trotted into Hopewell-on-Lyft, the last watering hole before the Sedgemere estate village.

"Shall we have a pint?" Sedgemere asked. "The summer ale at The Duke's Arms is exceptional, and tarrying here will give my staff a few extra moments to flutter about before they must once again deal with me."

Sedgemere wasn't particularly fond of ale, though he felt an obligation to give his custom to the inn when he passed through the area. The innkeeper and his wife were good folk, and the service excellent for so small an establishment.

Though a delay here meant the boys would have to wait longer to see their father, and their lack of patience never boded well for the king's peace—or Sedgemere's breakables.

"A pint and a plate here will do," Hardcastle said. "I'm in no hurry to complete any part of this journey."

"One wonders how will you corrupt my firstborn if you never see the boy. A pint and a plate it is."

"Mustn't forget to corrupt the future duke, the present one having become such a ruddy bore," Hardcastle said, brightening as much as he ever brightened. "I must see to the boy's education, and make a thorough job of it too. Several months should suffice."

"As if you'd winter in the—what the deuce?"

An altercation was in progress in the coaching yard of The Duke's Arms, between a sweating, liveried coachman and the head hostler, an estimable fellow named Helton.

"Gentlemen," Sedgemere said, swinging off his horse. "The day is too hot for incivilities. What is the problem?"

Hardcastle dismounted as well, though he—having only the one child in his nursery—knew little about sorting through disputes. The buffoonery of the House of Lords didn't signify compared to small boys in the throes of affronted honor.

"Your Grace." Helton uncrossed beefy arms and tugged a graying forelock. "Welcome to The Duke's Arms, Your Grace. My pardon for speaking too loudly. John Coachman and I was simply having a discussion."

John Coachman was another muscular individual of mature years, though in livery, the heat had turned him red as a Leicestershire squire's hunting pinks.

"Yon fellow refused me a fresh team," John Coachman snapped, "and this a coaching inn. I never heard the like, and my lady having had to make do with as sorry a foursome of mules as I ever cursed in my life for the past seven leagues."

The coach horses were not mules, but they were on the small side, a bay, a chestnut, and two dingy grays, and every one was heaving with exhaustion, their coats matted with dusty sweat.

"John?" came a feminine voice from around the side of the coach. "What seems to be the problem?"

Sedgemere's body comprehended the problem before his brain did, for he knew that voice. Brisk, feminine, and pitched a trifle lower than most women's, that was the voice of a few memorable dreams and one interesting encounter in Hyde Park nearly a week past.

"Miss Faraday," Hardcastle said, bowing and tipping his hat.

"Madam," Sedgemere said, doing likewise. "Your coach appears to be in need of a fresh team."

She wasn't wearing a bonnet, perhaps in deference to the heat, perhaps because she was indifferent to her complexion. Summer sunshine found red highlights in her dark hair, and the midday breeze sent curls dancing away from her face.

Desire paid an unexpected call on Sedgemere, a novel experience in broad daylight. His waking hours were spent avoiding the notice of the ladies, and thus he was usually safe from his own animal spirits. Miss Faraday, fortunately, was more interested in the horses than she was a pair of dukes idling in a rural coach yard.

"These four beasts have gone ten miles past a reasonable distance," she said. "I'll not be responsible for abusing them with the weather so miserable. If the inn hasn't any teams to spare—"

"You'll bide with me and Hardcastle for the space of a meal," Sedgemere said, while in the back of his mind, Alasdair—the Marquess of Ryland, rather— led his brothers on a shrieking nursery revolt. "By the time you've refreshed yourself, I'll have a team on the way from Sedgemere House."

"A fine plan," Hardcastle chorused on cue. "You must agree, Miss Faraday, it's a pretty day for a quiet meal in the shade, and Sedgemere has, in his inimitable style, solved every problem on every hand."

Hardcastle was laying it on a bit thick, but such was his habitual sincerity, or so oppressive was the heat, that Miss Faraday sent a longing glance to the oaks shading the inn.

"You're suggesting we dine *al fresco*?" she asked.

Insects dined *al fresco*. Birds came dodging down from the boughs to interrupt outdoor meals. Stray bits of pine needle found their way into the food. A father of three boys had firsthand experience with these and other gustatory delights.

"The breeze is lovely," Sedgemere said, drawing the lady away from the horses by virtue of tugging on her wrist. "The Duke's Arms has a pretty garden around to the side, and Hardcastle will be happy to place our order with the kitchen."

"I shall be ecstatic, of course," Hardcastle muttered, passing the reins of his horse to a stable boy. "You see before you a duke in raptures."

Sedgemere saw before him a duke half in love, which would not do. "Come along, Miss Faraday. Mr. Helton can send to Sedgemere House, and you'll be on your way in no time."

Helton bustled off, John Coachman bowed his overheated thanks, and Sedgemere led the only woman with whom he felt comfortable being private to the seclusion and sweet scents of the coaching inn's garden.

"My maid," Miss Faraday said, slipping her hand from Sedgemere's. "Carsdale has gone around to the—"

"The inn's goodwife will doubtless inform your maid of your location," Sedgemere said. "Many patrons avail themselves of the garden, if you're concerned for the appearances."

Miss Faraday was a beautiful woman, though contrary to current fashion, her hair was dark, her eyes were green, and her features were on the bold side. Her brows were particularly expressive, and Sedgemere happened to be studying them—mentally tracing them with his tongue, in fact—so he noticed when unexpected emotion flitted across Miss Faraday's features.

"I ought to be concerned for the appearances," she retorted. "You should know, Your Grace, I'm considering getting myself ruined."

"Lucky you," Sedgemere said, batting aside his ungentlemanly imaginings. "You *can* be ruined, while I am hopelessly ensnared in respectability, even if I wager irresponsibly, waste my days in opium dreams, and neglect my estates and my children."

Sedgemere had no experience with damsels in distress, but he suspected making them smile might be a good step toward slaying their dragons.

Miss Faraday refused to oblige him.

"I am half in earnest, Your Grace. Do not jest when I face days more travel. The last coaching inn gave us the same story. The Quality is off to the house parties, leaving London for the shires, and for me, no fresh team is available. If I didn't know better, I'd think somebody was traveling ahead, warning the inns not to spare me a single decent horse."

Sedgemere led the lady to the shade of the venerable oaks at the side of the inn. His attraction to her was inconvenient, but understandable. Her testiness around him made her safe. She was comely, and he was in the midst of one of his increasingly frequent periods of sexual inactivity.

Frequent and bothersome.

"You are tired," Sedgemere said. "You are vexed by the heat, your lady's maid has likely been complaining the entire distance from London, and you haven't had a decent meal for three days. Let's find a shady seat, Miss Faraday, and you can curse me, the Great North Road, and the summer heat, not in that order."

The scowl Miss Faraday turned on Sedgemere was magnificent. "Don't patronize me, Your Grace. I much prefer the disdain of my betters to anybody's condescension."

She reminded him of his cat, Sophocles, a temperamental soul who hissed first and apologized never. And yet, Sedgemere was always unaccountably pleased to be reunited with his cat, just as he was pleased to find himself thrown into company with Miss Faraday.

"Oh, very well," he said, opening a tall door in a taller stone wall. "*I* am vexed by the heat, *I* haven't had a decent meal for three days, and Hardcastle's whining and arguing have about driven *me* to Bedlam. Are you happy now, Miss Faraday?"

The daft woman was smiling at him, beaming at him as if he were Alasdair—Ryland, rather—and had just recited the entire royal succession perfectly.

"Effie was right," she said, which made no sense. "Come along, Your Grace. A hungry duke is not a patient creature."

She took him by the wrist and led him into the cooler confines of the shaded garden, where, as fate or a lucky duke would have it, not another soul was to be seen.

* * * * *

Sedgemere was a tease.

Anne marveled to reach this conclusion, but what else explained that slight warmth in his eyes, the affection with which he complained about His Grace of Hardcastle, or the way he'd invited her to curse him?

She preceded the duke into a garden redolent of honeysuckle and lush grass, for this was a cottage garden, not the manicured miniature park found behind the town houses in London's wealthy neighborhoods.

"I've never seen heartsease in such abundance," she said, as the duke closed the garden door. "And the lavender is exquisite." The border along the garden's south-facing wall was thick with silvery-green leaves and vibrantly-purple flowers.

"It's been years since I took a moment to tarry in this garden," Sedgemere said, taking off his hat. "There's as much delight here for the nose as for the eye, and the quiet pleases even the weary traveler's ear."

His pale hair was creased from his hat brim. Anne riffled the duke's hair back into order, as she would have with her papa.

"Better," she said. "Can't have you looking like John Coachman at the end of a hard morning's drive, Your Grace. I must have a whiff of that lavender."

Anne marched across the garden, expecting her escort to follow. Sedgemere remained in the shade near the gate, his hat in hand, his expression chilly indeed. Perhaps one didn't put a duke to rights, but Sedgemere would probably have expired of excessive dignity before running his hand through his own hair.

Anne plucked several sprigs of lavender, squeezing the flowers gently to release their scent. "Have you a penknife, Your Grace?"

He emerged from the shadows and passed her not a penknife, but a folding knife extracted from his boot.

"Don't you have outriders, lackeys, footmen, and such to carry arms for you?" Anne asked, cutting the lavender stems short.

"A duke is a target, Miss Faraday, and thus the duke himself should be armed at all times. Do you travel to your father's estate in Yorkshire?"

He meant he was a target for more than matchmakers. That the ducal person would be endangered by wealth and status had not occurred to her.

"Yorkshire is my final destination, and I hope Papa will join me there, but he takes his work seriously."

Anne had done it again, brought up her father's work early in a conversation. She must learn to be more careful around Sedgemere, though nobody else had noticed her tendency to mention commerce so readily.

"May I?" Sedgemere took the lavender from her and divided the bundle, passing half back to her. The remaining sprigs he attempted to tuck into the lapel of his riding jacket.

"Let me," Anne said, taking back the lavender and grasping the duke's lapel. "You'll break the stems, and it wants…"

She fell silent, fashioning an informal boutonnière for His Grace. Standing this close to him, she caught the scent of horse, exertion, and something like the garden itself. Private greenery and summer flowers, with the lavender note more prominent.

"There," she said, smoothing the shoulder of his jacket. "You're marginally presentable."

Anne was tall, but Sedgemere had nearly six inches on her. He stood gazing down the ducal proboscis, his expression much like it had been at the garden gate.

"I'm sorry," Anne said, stepping back, as heat rose up her neck that had nothing to do with the oppressive weather. "I don't mean to presume, but my father has long been widowed. I'm more than of age, and thus I'm the lady of his house. He'd go about half-dressed, a laughingstock, unless I took him in hand, and I don't—"

A single bare finger landed gently on Anne's lips.

"My own duchess," Sedgemere said, "who was very mindful of the appearances, never troubled herself over my attire. I am in your debt."

Was he teasing? Scolding? "You are not mocking me," Anne concluded. "Papa is frequently the object of ridicule. The titled gentlemen, and even some of the ladies, will call upon him, all of them in need of money. They do not respect him."

Too late, Anne recalled that Sedgemere had called on Papa too, more than once.

"Let us find a bench in the shade," Sedgemere said, placing Anne's hand on his arm. "I respect your father very much, and I suspect half the sneering, impecunious younger sons who seek his coin not only respect him, they fear him."

"Not only younger sons," Anne said. "Papa has been summoned to call upon more than one royal duke, Your Grace."

The duke found them a worn wooden bench beneath a spreading oak, where the fragrance of honeysuckle was thick in the air. Propriety was appeased by a clear view of the open doors that doubtless led to the inn's common.

"I enjoy puzzles," Sedgemere said, coming down beside her. "Two solutions present themselves to the riddle of why a royal duke would take tea with a lowly, if wealthy, banker. Your father was summoned to Clarence or Cambridge's parlor either to buy a minor title for himself or a lofty title for you."

How easily Sedgemere divined the disrespect that characterized all of Anne's days. "Well, no, actually. In exchange for the privilege of enduring an aging royal duke's intimate company, Papa would be considered for the honors list, for a sum certain."

The intimations had been delicate, but clear: Papa had been invited to *pay* to ensconce Anne as the mistress of a royal duke. She'd laughed when Papa had come home fuming and sputtering, poured Papa a brandy, and calmed him down, then gone to her room and sobbed into her pillow.

Sedgemere took Anne's hand when she would have bolted from the bench. "Your tale confirms what most of the realm has long suspected: With few exceptions, the present royal dukes are parasites and trollops. On their behalf, I apologize, Miss Faraday."

How had she got onto this subject, and why did Sedgemere's apology make her throat ache?

"Papa said the entire conversation progressed by innuendo and intimation, and that he might have been mistaken." He'd needed three brandies to concoct that bouncer.

"But he warned you nonetheless," Sedgemere said. "No wonder you have no patience with dukes or debutantes. You must consider the lot of us beneath your notice."

His hand was warm, and while Anne hadn't held hands with a man before, she suspected Sedgemere was good at it. The duke had the knack of a grasp that comforted rather than restrained, a gentle hold that was in no wise tentative.

"It's worse than that, Your Grace. I have no idea what to do with any of you. I can't afford to mistake a false smile for one that's genuine, I can't trust a gentleman to be a gentleman, I can't say the wrong thing, and thus even what I don't say becomes a means of judging me. I have decided that once I get home to Yorkshire, I will remain there. Papa can argue all he pleases, but I'm tired—"

Effie marched through the French doors, two serving maids behind her, the Duke of Hardcastle bringing up the rear. When Anne would have snatched her hand back, Sedgemere held firm, patted her knuckles, and only then allowed her to retrieve her hand.

"You have all the burdens of being a duchess," he said, "but none of the benefits. I know of this weariness you mention, Miss Faraday, and the longing to retire to the country, for it plagues me as well. Don't tell Hardcastle, though, for somebody must keep an eye on him in Town, and that somebody is me."

Sedgemere assisted Anne to her feet, while Hardcastle fussed the maids about where to spread the blanket, and Effie fussed generally. For a progression of astonished minutes, Anne remained arm in arm with the only titled person to ever, ever offer her kindness and understanding rather than judgment and ridicule.

* * * * *

"I think she likes me," Hardcastle said from his side of the picnic blanket. "I have an instinct about these things, and Miss Faraday likes me."

"She felt sorry for you," Sedgemere replied, brushing his fingers over the lavender scenting his lapel. "Your entire conversation dealt with your prodigy of a nephew, your prodigy of a horse, or your nephew's prodigy of a governess."

Sedgemere had been particularly interested to hear about this governess— Miss Ellen MacHugh—for Hardcastle's rhapsodies on her behalf sparked memories of similar flights from him over the past several years.

No wonder Hardcastle was so devoted to the family seat, poor sod.

"My nephew and my horse are very intelligent," Hardcastle retorted as the serving maids cleared away the detritus of the picnic. "Miss MacHugh is…"

Sedgemere let the silence lengthen. Miss Faraday had followed her maid inside, and the fresh team of horses had yet to arrive. The meal had been delightful, with Miss Faraday gently teasing Hardcastle, and Hardcastle's expression turning as dazed as Sedgemere felt.

"Miss MacHugh is… my nephew's governess," Hardcastle said. "The boy is devoted to her."

"You are a duke," Sedgemere replied as the last of the serving maids left them the privacy of the garden. "If you want to marry a governess, then marry her. Dukes have married serving maids, mistresses, commoners of every stripe. Marry your Miss MacHugh."

"Don't be daft. A duke must marry responsibly, or gossip will plague his duchess all of her days."

Sedgemere got to his feet, for a commotion beyond the garden walls suggested the new team was in the stable yard.

"That is your grandmother talking, Hardcastle. If *you* are plaguing your duchess all of her days and nights, and your duchess returns the compliment, what matters gossip?"

Hardcastle was off the blanket in one lithe movement, dusting at his breeches and tapping his hat onto his head.

"Your circumstances are different," Hardcastle said, pulling his riding gloves from a pocket. "You married quite well, your nursery is full, and the rest of your days *and nights* are your own to do as you see fit."

Where had Miss Faraday got off to, and what was Hardcastle hinting at? "I'm in no mood to repeat the error of my first marriage, Hardcastle. No more need be said on that matter."

Hardcastle had no graces, but he was brave, as all dukes needed to be. "Miss Faraday *likes* you too, Sedgemere. She's an heiress, she's pretty, she's situated not far from your family seat, and you are smitten. I can excuse you from the house party if you'd rather woo the fair maid this summer."

Sedgemere wandered over to the lavender border, cut off a fat bunch of sprigs, and stuffed them in his pocket. He wouldn't know how to woo Miss Faraday if she wrote him instructions. Dukes were excused from the wooing portion of a young man's education, which might explain why duchesses were a sour-natured lot.

"Miss Faraday is justifiably unimpressed with polite society," Sedgemere said, for Hardcastle had wandered right along beside him. "She longs for a life of peaceful spinsterhood, and has nothing but bad associations with titled men."

"*You* have nothing but bad associations with titled men *and* women," Hardcastle retorted, "present company excepted, I hope. What would it hurt to ride over to Yorkshire and see how she's getting on in a week or two?"

It would hurt, to see Miss Faraday happily ensconced at her father's lovely estate, relieved to be free of dukes, dowagers, and talk of her dowry.

"We have a house party to endure, Hardcastle, and Miss Faraday is intent on a repairing lease at her father's estate, if not a full retreat. I'd have better luck with your governess."

Dark brows drew down fiercely at that suggestion, while Miss Faraday emerged from the inn, her hair somewhat tidier.

Which made Sedgemere want to un-tidy it.

"I'll see to the horses," Hardcastle said, touching a finger to Sedgemere's boutonnière, then taking his leave of the lady.

Miss Faraday smiled at Hardcastle in parting, patted his shoulder, then his hand, and all the while, she didn't seem to know she was taking liberties with a ducal person. She'd spoken honestly, then. She was simply accustomed to life as her papa's companion, which struck Sedgemere as... wrong.

"Your Grace," she said, her smile dimming. "I must thank you for your company and for the loan of your team. I'll send John back with them within the week."

"No hurry. My stables are extensive, and I've plenty for my own needs." He also kept teams of his choosing at various coaching inns, as did Hardcastle. The loan of a team of horses was nothing to him.

"Do you even know how dismissive you sound?" she asked.

They were alone in the garden, and though they were in full view of the common, the midday hour had passed, and thus they had relative privacy for a few more minutes.

"I've cultivated the ability to dismiss with a word, a silence, a lifted eyebrow," Sedgemere said. "You have the same talent, though."

Ah, he'd surprised her. What a treat, to see confusion instead of a wariness in her eyes.

"I am not a duke, sir. I don't cultivate haughtiness."

Sedgemere leaned closer. "You, madam, have glowered at me from across a ballroom so loudly I was certain I had failed to button my falls, at the very least. Had perhaps even dribbled gravy on my cravat."

"I did that?" She was pleased with herself, as well she should be. "Are you certain I was looking at you? If you were standing near a royal duke, for example, or a certain viscount, or possibly—there's nearly a regiment of earls I avoid at all costs."

"So you turn that glower on us all," Sedgemere said, "and here I thought you cherished a special disdain for me. I'm crushed to know I merit not even your particular dislike, Miss Faraday."

Out in the inn yard, Helton called for the team to be backed into the traces. The time to part had arrived, and were Sedgemere another man, he would have admitted to anger. Miss Faraday would depart for Yorkshire, there to hide from polite society. He would travel on to the Lakes to dodge the matchmakers while keeping Hardcastle from their clutches as well.

What a waste of a lovely summer, and of a lovely woman with whom Sedgemere had found an odd commonality of interests.

"We should go," Miss Faraday said. "Where's your hat, Your Grace?"

"You truly have to manage your father, don't you?" Sedgemere said, retrieving his hat from a bench.

Miss Faraday's features arranged themselves into the expression he'd seen from her before. Banked distaste, not a sneer, more like controlled martyrdom.

"Papa is hopeless. People seek his counsel either because they need coin, or because they need to turn two coins into three. He helps as many as he can, but the interest he reaps is disrespect. He doesn't even see most of it, and has no idea why a man's cravat ought to be a basis for judging him."

They ambled into the shade, pausing before the closed garden door.

Sedgemere cast around for some encouraging words, some cheering sentiment he could leave Miss Faraday with. Her course was set: She would retire to the country, nurture her affronted dignity, and grow thorny roses—or something.

"What's the worst part of it?" he asked, settling his hat on his head. "What makes London unbearable?"

For London was the only place he was likely to see her, assuming she ever again ventured south.

"The money," she said, in the same tones somebody else might have referred to the scent downwind from a shambles. "People don't see me, they see the money. They resent it, they covet it, they gossip about it, and all I am is a means to that money. Papa doesn't understand. I didn't understand myself until the marriage proposals started."

From that pack of nasty, presuming earls, no doubt.

"For me, it's the title," Sedgemere said. He and the lady were parting, their paths likely would never cross again, and he could be honest with Anne Faraday as he wasn't honest with even Hardcastle. "I never wanted a damned title, much less a ducal title. I'm not a man, I'm a title, a deep pocket, consequence, estates."

"So," she said, straightening a wrinkle in his coat sleeve over his biceps, "you snarl and sneer, and arch the eyebrow of doom, lest any presume on your good nature. Good for you, sir. You're entitled to your privacy, and to deal with the world on your own terms."

Anne Faraday addressed him not as a duke, who endured toadying and deference without limit, but rather, as a man who'd put up with enough, and had a right to order his affairs as he saw fit. Nobody else had spoken to him thus. Nobody else had dared.

Nobody else had understood.

Sedgemere meant to kiss her cheek, truly he did. Maybe she meant to kiss his too, for when Sedgemere lowered his head, lips at the ready for a chaste—if bold—buss to her cheek, she presented her lips, also at the ready, and a kiss occurred.

Not a kiss to anybody's cheek, but a collision of lips, surprised at first, then curious, then… enthusiastic.

Wonderfully, lustily enthusiastic. Everything external fell away from Sedgemere's notice—the inn yard commotion beyond the garden wall, the clatter and clank of dishes from a kitchen window ten yards off, the lowing of a cow in the pasture behind the inn.

While everything inside Sedgemere, everything that brushed up against the slightest aspect of that kiss, woke up.

And rejoiced.

CHAPTER 3

Anne had three more days on the king's highway before she reached her destination, three days of jostling, bouncing, and ignoring Effie's prattle.

Three days and two nights of failing to find the right words to describe the Duke of Sedgemere's kiss. That single kiss had been surprising. Anne hadn't realized she was capable of flaunting convention to the extent of putting her lips on the ducal person.

And the surprises didn't stop there. Sedgemere's kiss intrigued, offering contradictions and complexities, like a business opportunity in a foreign culture. His kiss was confident without being arrogant, gentle without being chaste, ardent but respectful, intimate without presuming.

Anne would be a lifetime analyzing one kiss that for Sedgemere had probably been an unremarkable moment in a life of casual privilege and sophistication. He'd not even smiled at her, but rather, had handed her up into the coach, tipped his hat, and wished her safe journey.

"We're coming to the gates," Effie said. "Thank the Almighty, we're finally coming to the gates."

"Effie, you've never traveled in such comfort as you have the past three days," Anne said, for once the Duke of Sedgemere's first team of coaching horses had been put to, the hostlers at subsequent inns had replaced them with further loans of Sedgemere horses. Meals had arrived to Anne's rooms hotter and faster. Her chambers had been the best the premises had to offer.

The woman who became Sedgemere's duchess would have a lovely life, in some particulars.

"Traveling is traveling," Effie harrumphed. "And now we're to deal with the staff of a duke and duchess. Mark me, miss, they'll want their vales and be as high in the instep as the duke himself."

Veramoor's estate lay in the Lakes, snuggled right up against the Whinlatter forest. Anne had enjoyed the scenery, which was unlike even the sweeping green landscape of the Dales. She did not enjoy the prospect of the next two weeks. Communication with Papa would be difficult, for she'd brought only so many pigeons.

And Veramoor had doubtless invited a number of bachelor earls, for he and his duchess fancied themselves matchmakers.

"My, my, my," Effie whispered, gawking out the window. "It's a bloomin' palace, miss. You'll need a ball of twine to keep from getting lost between the bedroom and the breakfast parlor."

The façade was majestic, a massive Baroque structure that put Anne in mind of the Howard family seat in Yorkshire. Two enormous wings projected from a central dome, the whole approached by a long drive that ended in a broad carriageway encircling a fountain.

Thus did dukes live. The grandeur of Veramoor House was a reproach to any banker's daughter who longed for more kisses from chance-met dukes. Papa could afford such a dwelling, but neither he nor Anne would know what to *do* with it.

"I was wrong," Effie said as the carriage drew to a halt. "You'll need six balls of twine, miss. Promise you won't leave without me. If I get lost, there's no chance of anybody finding me in this palace."

"You'll be given a map, Effie," Anne said, as a liveried footman opened the carriage door and flipped down the steps. "And I won't leave without you."

Effie might not be the only person Anne knew, but she'd definitely be the only person Anne could trust here.

Inside the house, Anne was greeted by the duchess, a petite, fading redhead with snapping blue eyes. Despite the grandeur of the entrance hall, Her Grace commanded the entire cool, soaring space, ordering footmen this way, porters the other.

"Oh, my dear Miss Faraday," Her Grace said, taking Anne by both hands. "You are the image of your mama. May I call you Anne? You must not call me Margot, alas, or the other ladies will be scandalized, but your mama called me Margot long ago. She talked me into trying a cigar the year she made her bow, and I—a sensibly married woman at the time—have never been so sick in all my days."

The duchess's tone was welcoming, her grasp warm and firm, and yet, she was warning Anne too. Special favor might be shown, but Anne must not presume.

Not that she would, ever. She'd kissed a passing duke by chance and for three days, been plagued by his memory. Missed him even, when she'd yet to spend more than two hours in his company.

"I had not heard this about my mother," Anne said. "You must tell me more when time allows."

"Harrison will show you to your rooms," Her Grace said, "but before the mob descends, you'll take tea with me, won't you? I'll send a footman to collect you in an hour or so, and your maid can sneak in a nice lie-down. Will that suit?"

The Duchess of Veramoor would not have taken three days to deal with matters at Waterloo. She'd have dispatched the Corsican by noon on the first day and been entertaining callers for luncheon thereafter, not a hair out of place.

"Tea would suit wonderfully, Your Grace. My thanks."

Sedgemere's teams must have made good time, because Harrison, an underhousekeeper, told Anne she was among the first to arrive. Most of the guests would be along as the day progressed, with more arriving tomorrow.

"And there are always stragglers." Harrison was a tall blonde who moved at a brisk pace, a set of keys jangling at her waist, a touch of Ireland in her words. "Her Grace never plans much for the first day, but we've high hopes for this year's gathering."

Anne had high hopes she'd be allowed to snatch a nap before her tea with the duchess. "I'm sure we'll all have a lovely time."

Until the gentlemen arrived and started bothering the maids, drinking too much, making inane wagers, and ogling Anne's bosom.

"Our record is four engagements," Harrison said, unfastening her keys. "That was three years ago, and one of them doesn't really count because it was Their Graces' youngest. Gave us a start, that one did, but she's wed happily enough and is expecting her second. Do you fancy any particular gentlemen?"

Merciful days. Longing shot through Anne's weariness, yearning for a quiet, fragrant walled garden, and a duke who was brusque, kind, and a surprisingly adept kisser.

"I beg your pardon?" Anne managed.

"Their Graces pride themselves on knowing when a couple might suit," Harrison said, thrusting a key into a lock. "They make up the guest list with the young people in mind, if you take my meaning. Her Grace says I talk too much, but you seem like the sensible sort."

"Thank you, though right now I'm the tired and dusty sort. This is a lovely room."

Early afternoon light flooded a cozy sitting room, one appointed in blue-and-gilt flocked wallpaper, blue and white carpets, blue velvet upholstered furniture, and bouquets of red and white roses. The impression was restful and elegant, and the blue and white decorating scheme carried into an airy adjoining bedroom.

"Her Grace puts her special guests on this corridor," Harrison said. "You have the best views and the most quiet. The bell pull is near the privacy screen, and a tray will be sent along shortly. We'll have a buffet tonight. Guests gather at seven in the blue gallery. Any footman or maid can give you directions."

No balls of twine, alas. Harrison went bustling on her way, Effie disappeared to locate Anne's trunks, and for the first time in days, Anne was in the midst of complete silence.

So, of course, memories of Sedgemere's kiss resonated only more loudly. Of his gloved hand cupping her cheek, his tongue brushing over her bottom lip, his leg insinuated between her thighs.

"If I'm to have only one forbidden kiss in my life, that one will at least linger in memory until I forget my own name," Anne murmured. She twitched a lacy curtain back and cracked open the window. Her room overlooked the side of Veramoor House that faced the stables, magnificent buildings that might well have been lodging for another titled family.

Carriage houses sat beside the stables, and green paddocks stretched behind them up to the slope of the woods. A woman of artistic talent would gorge herself on views like this, while Anne's imagination went to the expense of such a facility.

That too had been in Sedgemere's kiss, a sense of wealth leading back across the centuries, tens of thousands of acres of tradition and stability, not merely a pile of newly minted coins. Sedgemere's kiss spoke of resources so vast, the man with title to them could dispense with time in any manner he saw fit, even if that meant indulging in a pointless kiss with a woman who should not have presumed on his time, much less his person.

"I'm not sorry I did it," Anne said. "I hope he's not sorry either."

Carriages tooled away from the main drive and over to the carriage houses, and grooms bustled about while porters transferred baggage to carts. Papa would need to know of Anne's safe arrival, and he'd doubtless send her dispatches requiring immediate replies.

Anne allowed herself one more moment at the window, one more moment to inhale a breeze scented by the nearby forest, the extensive gardens, and the magnificent stables. This was what a duchess's world smelled like of a summer, and it was lovely.

Another carriage made the trek from driveway to carriage houses, two horsemen riding ahead. The horses under saddle were beautiful animals, but their heads were down, their legs dusty. Both men dismounted, both took off their hats and gloves, both handed horses off to grooms.

Between one flutter of the lacy curtain and the next, Anne's mind confirmed three things that her abruptly pounding heart already knew.

First, the tall gentleman with the moonlight-blond hair was Sedgemere.

Second, if Anne were prudent, she'd never ever be alone with him again.

Third, if she did happen to find herself private with the duke in the next two weeks, she'd be helpless not to kiss him again—every chance she got.

* * * * *

"I say we should have arrived late," Hardcastle groused. "We ought to have tarried an extra day at Sedgemere, so you might have gone calling on a pretty neighbor in Yorkshire. But no, you are Sedgemere, so you heed no counsel save your own, and all creation must align itself for your convenience. You finally meet a woman who's up to your mettle, and instead of bestirring yourself to pique her interest, you lend her the fastest teams in the realm to speed her away from your side."

Hardcastle was nervous. Next he'd be spouting Latin, for that was how Hardcastle coped with the anxieties a bachelor duke must never exhibit before others.

"I say we needed to arrive early," Sedgemere replied, because short of Latin, a good argument settled Hardcastle's nerves. "One wants to scout the territory, befriend the help, study the maps, as it were. Veramoor is all genial bonhomie, but do not turn your back on his duchess."

"One doesn't," Hardcastle retorted, tugging at a cravat that had become dusty hours ago. "Not unless one is abysmally ill-mannered. What are you staring at?"

"Those are my blacks," Sedgemere said as a team of four coach horses was led around to the carriage bays, where the harness would be removed, polished, and carefully hung. "I know my own cattle, and those are my blacks."

"You must own two hundred black horses," Hardcastle said, withdrawing a flask and uncapping it. "One set of equine quarters looks the same as another."

"The heat has provoked you to blaspheming, and I know that team. I bought them from a Scottish earl not a year past, the first transaction I've done with the man. He brews a beautiful, lethal whisky."

"All whisky is lethal. They are a handsome team."

They were, in fact, a gorgeous team, for they confirmed that traveling the length of England with Hardcastle had not cost Sedgemere his few remaining wits. The coach from which the horses had been unhitched looked familiar because it *was* familiar.

When last Sedgemere had seen that coach, his entire being had yet been humming with the pleasure of having kissed the lady he'd just sent on her way at a tidy gallop.

"I do not care for that expression, Sedgemere," Hardcastle said, using a wrinkled handkerchief to bat the dust from his hat. "That expression is *bemused*, as if you're plotting mischief unbecoming of a gentleman. The last time I saw that expression, Headmaster nearly wore out his arm warming our little backsides."

"It was worth it," Sedgemere said. "We agreed the birching was worth seeing Lord Postlethwaite shorn of his flowing tresses for the rest of the term. Besides, what boy of eleven is vain about his hair, for God's sake? Poodlethwaite had it coming."

The nickname had been Hardcastle's stroke of genius. Sedgemere had been the one to cut off his slumbering little lordship's hair.

"Let's greet our host and hostess, shall we?" Hardcastle said. "I'm for a soaking bath and a nap, and I daresay you could use some freshening as well."

"Happens you're right." For as the handsome blacks were led away for a rubdown and some hours at grass, Sedgemere knew three things.

First, he would not present himself to Miss Faraday in all his dirt, though he would find her, and soon.

Second, he was a gentleman, so he must apologize for having kissed her.

Third, he most definitely would kiss her again, every chance he got.

* * * * *

"Those are children," Anne said, half of her weariness falling away. "I didn't realize the house party was to include children."

"Their Graces have thirty-six grandchildren, though the duchess's goal is one hundred," Harrison said. "The children are always welcome at Veramoor House."

Three little boys came to a halt facing Anne in the corridor. Each had flaming red hair, each carried a small valise.

"Ma'am," the tallest said, executing a bow. The other two bowed as well, but as a unit. Twins, then, though their looks were not exactly identical.

"Gentlemen," Anne said, curtseying. "Hello, I'm Miss Anne Faraday."

The shorter two exchanged a look. The tallest switched his valise from one hand to the other. "You're not Lady Anne? We only know ladies and servants."

"That was rude, Ryland," one of the twins said. "We know some commoner women who aren't servants. They aren't as pretty you though, ma'am."

The footman who'd been herding the boys along the corridor cleared his throat. Harrison twitched at her keys.

"Thank you for the compliment," Anne said to the shorter boy. "I am a commoner, but I'm also a guest at this house party. I hope you are too?"

The child who'd spoken not a word yet nodded and blushed, and because he was a redhead, his blush was brilliant, right to the tips of his ears.

"We're to help protect Hardcastle from the mamas and debutantes," Ryland said. "His Grace of Hardcastle told us so. I'm Alasdair, and this is Ralph and Richard. They're lords too."

More bows. Anne would explain proper introductions to them some time when two other adults weren't looking pained and impatient, and a duchess wasn't waiting tea on Anne.

"I am very pleased to meet you all," Anne said. "I hope our paths cross again soon. Will you stay for the full two weeks?"

"Oh, yes," Richard replied, "and we're not to get dirty ever, and we're to stay out of sight all the time, and we're to behave, or Papa will make us write Latin until Michaelmas. I don't see how we can help protect Hardcastle if we're doing all this behaving and staying out of sight."

The quiet boy, Ralph, spoke up in tones barely above a whisper. "Richard is l-logical. Papa is logical too."

Alasdair swatted Ralph's arm. "Ralph is our lexicon, when he talks at all."

Something quacked in the vicinity of Ralph's valise. Harrison's keys fell silent. The footman's eyebrows climbed nearly to the molding.

"I daresay you're all three tired and hungry," Anne said. "Best get up to the nursery soonest."

"Of course," the footman said, marching off. "Come along, your lordships."

"A pleasure to have met you," Anne said, curtseying as deeply as if they were three little dukes.

Alasdair, who was apparently burdened with a courtesy title already, bowed, followed by his brothers.

"Likewise, ma'am. Have a pleasant stay. Will you help us protect Hardcastle? Papa says friends look out for one another, and Hardcastle is my god-papa."

"He's quite fond of us too," Richard said. "He said so, anyway, and Papa didn't correct him."

For small children, these three could be quite serious, putting Anne in mind of...

Oh, merciful days. Hardcastle was Sedgemere's friend, and these were Sedgemere's boys. The blue eyes shaded closer to periwinkle rather than frozen sky, the noses were understated compared to His Grace's, but the earnestness, the gravity was already there.

"Assisting you to look out for the Duke of Hardcastle will be my special privilege," Anne said. "Do you see that door there, with the two birds on it? That is my room, and you may seek me there before supper if you have need of me. I'll know I can find you in the nursery."

Another quack issued from Ralph's valise. He clutched his traveling case to his chest, expression panicked. Richard and Alasdair stepped in front of him, the eldest wearing a scowl worthy of a duke.

"Off with you," Anne said, smiling brilliantly. "The Duchess of Veramoor is expecting me for tea, and I dare not disappoint her. Very pleased to have met you, gentlemen, and I look forward to seeing more of you."

When the footman nearly dashed up the stairs, the boys bolted after him, while Anne stood listening to indignant quacking that boded wonderful adventures for the next two weeks.

* * * * *

"I ought to see to the boys," Sedgemere said, though he'd rather accost an underbutler and bribe Miss Faraday's location out of him.

At Sedgemere's side, Hardcastle trudged up the stairs. "You ought to take a damned bath. Your fragrance is most un-ducal, Sedgemere. The boys will want a trip to the garden after having been cooped up in the coach all day, and they do not need you spouting lectures about *cave quid dicis*—well, hello, Miss

Faraday."

Beware what you say. Excellent advice at all times. Even knowing Miss Faraday was a guest at Veramoor House, Sedgemere wasn't prepared for the sight of her right there on the first landing of the main staircase. He was dusty, disheveled, and, yes, sweaty, while she was comfortably elegant in lavender sprigged muslin.

She was also staring at his mouth and smiling a pleased, naughty smile.

"Your Graces, good afternoon," she said, dipping a curtsey. "I believe I just had the pleasure of meeting your children, Sedgemere, and what delightful gentlemen they are."

Damn and blast. "They are hellions, madam, and don't be fooled by Lord Ralph's quiet either. I'll order them to stay away from you, not that children should be in adult company if it's at all avoidable. Veramoor was insistent that the children be brought along, and his duchess likes children, if you can credit such a thing."

He was babbling, and he stank, and Hardcastle was looking amused. Worse than all that, Miss Faraday's smile had disappeared.

"I like children," she said. "Like them better than most adults, and longed for siblings when I was growing up. I still wish I had a brother or a sister. Your sons are perfectly charming, and you should be proud to show them off."

Charm. Why the devil did women set so much store by charm? "If you say so," Sedgemere replied.

"He'll be taking the boys for a romp in the garden in about an hour," Hardcastle said, the wretch. "Perhaps you'd care to join them? This far north, the roses last a bit longer, and the light is lovely."

That was not Latin. That was Hardcastle meddling, though thank goodness, his bumbling had restored Miss Faraday's smile.

"A walk in the garden would be just the thing," she said. "From my window, I can see a fountain in a knot garden. Shall I meet you and the children there in an hour?"

Gardens and Miss Faraday were a lovely combination. "I'm not sure if the children—"

Hardcastle coughed, sounding like Sedgemere's own grandmama, then muttering something that sounded like *ducal dumbus doltus.*

"An hour," Sedgemere said. "Give or take. The boys struggle with punctuality." Also with manners, proper dress, deportment, French, Latin, sums—they were terrible with sums, the lot of them—and with anything resembling civility.

And yet, Sedgemere couldn't bring himself to send Alasdair—Ryland—off to Eton. Not just yet.

"I'll look forward to joining you." Miss Faraday patted Sedgemere's arm and bustled off, sending a whiff of lavender and loveliness though Sedgemere's tired brain.

"*Non admirentur,*" Hardcastle said. "And particularly don't gawk at the lady on the main staircase, when anybody might see you."

Sedgemere took the remaining stairs two at a time. "I'm to meet her in the garden in one hour, Hardcastle. That leaves me only thirty minutes to bathe, shave, and change, and thirty minutes to lecture the boys. Ten minutes per boy is hardly sufficient for putting them on their manners."

Hardcastle ascended the stairs at a maddeningly decorous pace. "The point of turning children loose in a huge garden is so they can for one quarter of an hour forget their manners. *You* certainly did."

"I beg your pardon?"

Hardcastle marched right past Sedgemere, heading down the long corridor on the side of the house overlooking the stables.

"You heard me," Hardcastle said. "At The Duke's Arms. I thought to retrieve you from the garden because Miss Faraday's coach was ready to leave the yard, and what do I find, but a peer of the realm accosting an innocent young lady in the shade. I withdrew quietly in deference to the lady's sensibilities *and my own.*"

"She gave as good as she got, Hardcastle. You mustn't be jealous."

"I am not jealous," Hardcastle said, counting doors as they strode along. "I am firmly in Miss Faraday's camp, and shall do all in my power to further her interests. I am confident the boys can be won to that cause as well. If your intentions with respect to Miss Faraday are dishonorable, I shall kill you. This is my room. Yours is the one with the rose carved on the door."

"You intrude on one kiss, and you're ready to call me out?" Sedgemere said, oddly touched.

"I'll shoot to kill. I'll take good care of the boys," Hardcastle replied. "You needn't worry on that score. I might marry Miss Faraday too."

Hardcastle was a bloody good shot, and he wasn't smiling, but then, Hardcastle never smiled.

"One kiss does not a debauch make," Sedgemere said. "I must away to my bath."

"Elias, for God's sake, be careful," Hardcastle said, jamming a key into the lock on his door. "You married young, and thus were spared the dangerous waters of infatuation and flirtation. Miss Faraday is decent, and your kisses could ruin her. You don't want the ruin of a young lady on your conscience, particularly not that young lady. Moreover, I do not want to raise your children."

Hardcastle's admonition was appropriate. A desire to kiss a woman wasn't that unusual, but Sedgemere's regard for *this* woman was something altogether more substantial.

"I won't ruin her," he said, fishing his own key from his pocket. "I like her, I like her father, and I have reason to hope she might like me. Let's leave it at that, shall we?"

Because tempus was fugit-ing, and a gentleman was punctual. Sedgemere had told the boys as much on hundreds of occasions.

"Be off with you," Hardcastle said, pushing his door open. "Perhaps later I'll explain to you the peculiar circumstances under which Lord Ralph asked me how to say 'duck' in Latin."

"Ralph is a quiet fellow with two brothers, both of whom are quick with their fists," Sedgemere said, fiddling the key in his lock. "Of course he needs to know how to duck in several languages."

Hardcastle shook his head and disappeared into his room.

The key turned in Hardcastle's lock, an appreciated reminder that cut through Sedgemere's sense of urgency. House-party rules meant bedroom doors stayed locked at all times. He'd make sure Miss Faraday grasped that thoroughly the next time he had enough privacy with her to kiss her senseless.

* * * * *

Tea with the duchess had been forty-five minutes of stories about Anne's mama, stories her own father hadn't seen fit to pass along, or perhaps Papa didn't know them.

Mama had apparently been an accomplished flirt, including foreign princes among her entourage, though she'd been the mere daughter of a baron. The idea that she could have married anybody, but had chosen Papa was... touching.

Anne had barely five minutes to stop by her room for a straw hat before finding her way to the knot garden, which was deserted. She forbade herself to check the time, and instead opened the first of the dispatches from Papa that had been waiting for her at Veramoor House.

The news was not good, but then, Papa was a worrier, taking the welfare of each client very much to heart, though he never, *ever* mentioned clients by name. Anne was mentally composing her reply when a shadow fell across the page.

"The Vandal horde will descend in less than five minutes. If that correspondence is valuable, you'd best tuck it away or they'll use it to start a conflagration and tell you they're re-enacting the burning of Moscow."

Sedgemere stood glowering down at her, though Anne hadn't heard his approach. She stashed Papa's epistle in her reticule and rose.

"Your Grace, good afternoon." Now what to say to him? Papa's stack of letters was a reminder that two weeks in the country was as much time as Anne would ever have for a flirtation with any man, much less the duke. Papa needed her, and always would.

"Hardcastle threatened to call me out for kissing you," he said, offering his arm. "I claim the same privilege. If he imposes his attentions on you contrary to your preferences, I will kill him."

Sedgemere's tone was colder than the Russian winter, and yet, Anne had the sense he spoke in jest. She accepted his escort and let him lead her away from the clipped symmetry of the knot garden.

"I can't imagine His Grace of Hardcastle imposing his attentions on anybody," Anne said. "He seems a shy fellow."

Sedgemere's hand rested over Anne's, probably the courtesy of a man who'd been married for several years. She liked most married men, for they tended to strut less and laugh more genuinely.

"Hardcastle will call *you* out, madam, if you tell anybody else he's shy, but he is. He inherited the title early, and natural circumspection became severe reticence as he matured. I would like to kiss you again, though, so tell me now if my attentions are unwelcome."

Merciful days. Was this how the nobility went about their affairs? Anne was spared from a reply by shrieking from the direction of Veramoor House's back terrace.

"Right on schedule," Sedgemere said, tensing. "I apologize in advance for the noise, the dirt, the lack of manners, the—"

"Over here!" Anne called, tugging off her straw hat and waving it. "Gentlemen, you've found us!"

Three little boys came pelting across the garden, Hardcastle following at a more decorous pace.

"Papa! We said we'd find you, and we did," the oldest called. "We found you in the first instant. Hello, Miss Anne!"

"Hello, Miss Anne!" Lord Richard chorused, elbowing Lord Ralph, who mumbled something.

"Apologize for your noise," Sedgemere bit out. "If a single guest thought to nap after a long day's travel, you've just woken them. You've probably spooked half the horses in His Grace's stables and curdled tomorrow's milk into the bargain. Ryland, I expect better of you."

Three little faces fell, three stricken gazes went to the crushed shells of the walkway. Clearly, Sedgemere himself was in need of a nap.

"But you did find us," Anne said. "And you're exactly on time, and you've brought His Grace of Hardcastle with you, which was very gracious of you. Might I trouble one of you gentlemen to put my hat on that bench by the roses? The sun is lovely after I've been shut up in a stuffy coach for days."

"I'll do it!" Richard yelled.

"I'd be pleased to assist you, ma'am," Ryland said, stepping in front of Richard.

"Perhaps Lord Ralph could tend to this errand for me," Anne said. "While Lord Ryland can find me six perfect daises, and you, Lord Richard, can scout us a patch of clover. I feel the need for some lucky clovers today, and I know just the sharp-eyed boys who can help me find them."

Three gallant little knights flung bows at her, then scampered off on their quests, while Hardcastle appropriated a bench some yards away.

"How did you do that?" Sedgemere asked. "You got them to bow, they're not bellowing, and nobody started a fight."

"We all like to feel useful, Your Grace." In Papa's household, Anne was endlessly useful, which was no comfort at all, weighed against the prospect of Sedgemere's kisses.

"I loathe being useful," Sedgemere said. "I'm useful from the moment I wake to the moment I close my eyes, tending to this estate, that committee, dodging the Regent's subtle requests for money. Usefulness can be wearing."

Out of the mouths of dukes…

"Little boys like to be useful, sir, and they were punctual, and they're very dear," Anne said, towing the duke past delphiniums the same shade of blue as his sons' eyes.

"Are you perhaps late to an engagement, Miss Faraday? We're required by propriety and common sense to remain within sight and sound of the boys. Their nursery maids, whom you will note are only now emerging onto the terrace, will be in a dazed stupor for the next three days. At least one of them will try to hand in her notice before facing the return journey."

Anne slowed her steps, though she'd been hauling His Grace in the direction of some shade provided by a pergola laden with grape vines.

"The boys need to run and make noise, Your Grace, while I, having surrendered my hat, need the shade."

"I am jealous of my offspring," the duke muttered. "For they get to do as they please, while you've yet to give me permission to share further kisses with you."

"You are very persistent," Anne said as they reached the shade. The arbor offered a view of the flowering beds and of three small boys, all crawling around in the grass in search of Anne's luck.

"I am very… interested in your kisses, Miss Faraday."

If Sedgemere opened a discussion of money, of pretty gifts offered as a token of his *interest*, Anne would be sick all over the heartsease.

Though she would be tempted. Papa wouldn't blame her, but the notion of becoming Sedgemere's mistress was… wretchedly tempting. Two weeks abruptly became an interminable sentence to disappointment and awkwardness.

Anne set aside her reticule, which held three fat letters from Papa. "I did not guard my virtue from all the impecunious viscounts and foul-breathed barons so I could sell it to you, Sedgemere. One kiss, no matter how lovely, doesn't earn you that much presumption, duke or no duke."

She took a seat. He remained standing, hands behind his back. Anne expected him to stomp away, taking his consequence, his presumption, and his kisses with him. She had a handkerchief in her reticule, and the vines roofing the arbor meant she could cry here in peace.

"I have insulted you," Sedgemere said. "That was not my intent." Still, he remained by the bench, like the clouds of a summer tempest hung over a valley, hoarding rain while flashing fire in the sky and threatening thunder from a distance.

"Do not loom over me. I'm tired, and I have correspondence to tend to, and surely, we needn't create drama so early in the gathering." Anne had warned Papa a house party was nothing but a waste of time.

"I'm waiting for you to invite me to share that bench, madam, so that we might have a civil discussion regarding your egregious misconception."

His tone said waiting was a significant imposition too.

"Do sit," Anne said, waving a hand. She'd forgotten her gloves in her haste to meet Sedgemere in the knot garden. The house party wasn't formal, so no great scandal would result from her oversight.

Sedgemere came down beside her like a hot air balloon drifted to earth, all slow, inexorable shadows, growing larger as he came closer. He chose to sit *quite* close to her.

"You have been propositioned by royalty," he said. "My apologies for creating the impression that—hell. I meant you no insult, Miss Faraday. I'm out of the habit of being attracted to a woman, any woman, and your kiss took me by surprise."

"As yours did me, Your Grace. Are you attracted to men?" Anne had two good male friends who escorted her regularly to the theater or the opera, though her primary function in their company was to quell gossip and enjoy the outing.

"You're not even supposed to know of such goings-on," Sedgemere said. "I will speak directly, because any minute, Ralph will bloody Richard's nose, Ryland will pummel Ralph, or Richard will black Ryland's eye."

"If you proposition me, I will do worse than that to you, Your Grace."

The look he gave Anne was appraising, or just possibly, approving. "I am forewarned. Please recall that Hardcastle must shoot me when you're done thrashing me. Wooing you will be exciting."

CHAPTER 4

"*Wooing me?*" Anne retorted. Pleasure, incredulity, and despair wafted on the fragrant breeze. "You barely know me, sir."

She and his grace sat side by side, nearly touching, though in the next moment Anne realized that the warmth covering her knuckles was Sedgemere's hand. Nobody would see him taking such a liberty, but Anne felt that touch everywhere.

"I like what I know of you so far," he said, "which is unusual enough that I'm interested in getting to know you better. Notice, I am not propositioning you, for which you'd beat me, and I am not proposing, for which you'd laugh me to scorn. I am suggesting that we use the next two weeks to become better acquainted. I've never met such a violent woman. Your passionate nature attracts me, if you must know."

Sedgemere's fingertips traced along the back of Anne's hand, the opposite of violence, his touch warm in contrast to his cool tone of voice.

"I've never been accused of having a passionate nature," Anne said. "Quite the contrary, until I met you." Papa used to call her his little abacus. Now she was stealing kisses in gardens, and nearly holding hands with Sedgemere in broad daylight. "I am not interested in marriage, Your Grace. My father's household is my home."

Though lately, that home felt more like a prison.

Sedgemere's fingers paused, then wandered to the underside of Anne's wrist and from there to her palm. His touch was neither presuming nor hurried, and yet, all of Anne's attention was riveted to the question of where his fingers would travel next.

"Then perhaps," he said, "over the next two weeks, I can change your mind, hmm? Perhaps you'll consider your options, and include me among them. Or perhaps you won't."

A breeze stirred the vines above, bringing the scent of the stable and forest beyond. Beneath those hearty, earthy scents was the fragrance the duke wore, which Anne would ever associate with tender, surprising kisses.

"I won't change my mind," Anne said. "I might…"

Sedgemere's fingers laced with hers, like vines embowering a bench beneath a trellis, lovely to look at, but strong enough to tear down stone edifices, given enough summers.

"Yes, Miss Faraday?"

"I will not marry you, and I will not be your mistress."

Across the garden, a boy yelled about having *found one*.

"Those parameters exactly define the bounds of a thorough wooing," Sedgemere said, leaning close. "If you think you've dissuaded me from further kisses, you are daft."

He kissed her cheek and rose just as Lord Ralph came churning into the arbor.

"I found one!" he bellowed. "Miss Far Away, I f-found one."

"Her name—" Sedgemere began as Anne shot to her feet and approached the boy.

"Lord Ralph, you must show me. It's been an age since I've even seen a four-leaf clover, and you've brought this one straight to me."

Anne knelt and admired a big, perfect four-leaf clover. "Come," she said, taking a blushing Lord Ralph by the hand. "We must show your papa."

"But your name—" Sedgemere said as Anne led the boy to his father.

She glowered at the duke, brandishing her lucky clover. Her smile promised that if Sedgemere tromped on Lord Ralph's accomplishment, there'd be no more shared kisses, not on any terms.

"This is the most magnificent clover I have ever seen," she said, shoving it before Sedgemere's eyes. "Don't you agree, Your Grace?"

Sedgemere closed his hand over Anne's, more warmth, more strong, sure wrapping of his fingers around a part of her person. She kept hold of the boy with her other hand, which left her no means by which to hang on to her wits.

"That is…" Sedgemere's brows drew down, brows very like those on little Ralph. "That is a fine clover. I'm sure it's redolent of good luck."

"It's green," Ralph said.

"Redolent is not a color," Sedgemere began. "The word comes from the Latin verb *redolēre*—"

Because Anne was out of hands, she nudged Sedgemere's boot with her toe. "Of course it's green. Your papa means that this clover reeks of luck." She took a sniff, then held the clover under the ducal nose. "It's lovely, wouldn't you agree, Your Grace?"

Sedgemere took a cautious whiff. "I have never smelled a luckier clover, Miss Faraday."

Ralph's smile was bashful. "I found it myself."

"Then you must keep it," Anne said, dropping the boy's hand. "This is the most special lucky clover I've ever seen, and you found it."

Anne could feel Sedgemere's lectures ready to rain down, about gentlemanly generosity, *trifolium whatever-um*, and grass-stained knees, of which Ralph had two.

"You must keep it, Miss Faraday," Ralph said. "I found it for you."

Anne fluttered, she gushed, she sniffed at the clover, then thanked Ralph from the bottom of her heart, while Sedgemere shifted from boot to boot. When Ralph had galloped back to the clover patch, Anne fetched her reticule off the bench and tucked the clover between the folds of one of Papa's letters.

"Don't you dare," she said to His Grace, "tell me Ralph is a silly little child. He's a fine boy, and he brought me a lovely clover. He got my name wrong the first time only because he was excited, you see, and if you must inflict Latin on him, then you make it special, a secret he shares only with you. He's a small boy, not a duke, so you must speak English to him, not duke-ish."

"Miss Faraday."

Anne jerked the strings of her reticule closed. "Thank you for a lovely outing, Your Grace. I will take my leave of their young lordships before I go in."

"Madam."

Anne had to get away. Had to answer Papa's letters before she tore them to bits. Sedgemere wanted to woo her, while she wanted… children, a husband, a home of her own. Mundane blessings every girl was raised to treasure.

"*Anne.*"

She looked around for her hat, then realized the tongue-tied Lord Ralph had left it halfway across the garden at her request.

"Your Grace?"

He drew her to the back of the arbor, a shady, private place where a lady could gather her composure.

"My son, my Ralph, who barely says a word if his twin is in the same room, is now standing a full two inches taller because of you and your silly clover. He spoke to you in sentences. I heard him, and if you only knew how long… he's shy."

Sedgemere's words were entirely understandable, but he'd again acquired the quality of a storm cloud, billowing with emotions, raising the wind, lightning visible, thunder threatening, and yet not a drop of his finer sentiments hit the earth.

Insight struck like a thunderclap. "You worried about him," Anne said. "You're smart enough as a parent to worry about the child who's quiet."

"*I* was quiet," Sedgemere said, jamming his hands into his pockets. "A ducal heir cannot *be* quiet. He must be studious, though practical. Intelligent, but not academic. Well-read, without being bookish. He must command the respect of all, while trusting none."

"He sounds like a very dull creature," Anne said slowly, "a miserable creature. Lord Ralph is three removes from the title, though." In the next instant, she knew, simply from the set of Sedgemere's jaw, that *he* had been three removes from the title too, and the progression from younger son or nephew to duke had been miserable and dull indeed.

Also lonely.

"Oh, Sedgemere." Anne wrapped her arms around him and hugged him as tightly as she'd wanted to hug Ralph when he'd brought her his clover. "I'm sorry."

Hugging Sedgemere was like hugging a surveying oak, like trying through weightless emotion to sway a landmark valued for its very immobility. Anne hugged him anyway, grateful for the sheltering privacy of the grape arbor.

Sedgemere was not a monument to ducal consequence and titled self-importance. He was a papa consumed with worry, and trying, by Latin and lectures, to safeguard children who'd someday have to muddle on without him.

"My mother taught me numbers," Anne said, resting her cheek against Sedgemere's lacy cravat. "She was desperate for me to learn numbers, because Papa is a banker, and without numbers, I'd have no way to understand him. I don't hate the numbers, but I'd rather have more memories of my mother, not my math teacher."

A hand landed on Anne's hair, gentle as sunbeams. "Hardcastle says the same thing. He lost his parents, and wishes not that his father had had more time to show him how to be a duke, but rather, had had more time to show him how to go on with the present ducal heir. Little children come without instructions. A grievous disservice to those raising them."

And to the small boys and girls.

Sedgemere's arms had stolen around Anne, and she remained in his embrace, the benevolent breeze whispering through the greenery around them, honeysuckle gracing the moment. This was not kissing, but Anne most assuredly felt wooed.

"They'll be back," Sedgemere said, "and not a four-leaf clover will survive in Veramoor's gardens."

"We must treasure the ones we come upon today," Anne said, "or over the next two weeks, for they might be all the lucky clovers we shall ever find."

Sedgemere stepped back, a trailing vine of grape leaves brushing his crown. "You'll give me two weeks, then? Two weeks to win your friendship, and whatever else I might entice from you?"

Dalliance was the name for what lay between the mercenary interest of a mistress and the marital commitment of a wife. Temporary passion, stolen moments, lovely memories.

Bearable heartbreak.

More than Anne had ever thought to have, much less than she wished for, and probably far less than Sedgemere intended.

"A ducal dalliance," she said. "Those must be the best kind."

His gaze cooled, suggesting Anne had disappointed him. That hurt, but leaving him at the end of two weeks would hurt more. Never kissing him again, never tasting his passion, or hearing his confidences again, would have hurt most of all.

* * * * *

Sedgemere chatted, socialized, and was amiable, in so far as he was capable of such nonsense, all the while intercepting debutantes intent upon making off with Hardcastle's bachelorhood. The job was taxing, when what Sedgemere preferred to do was spend time with Miss Anne Faraday.

The boys, oddly enough, provided the means to achieve that end, for Miss Faraday liked children.

Because Sedgemere liked *her*, that meant he too spent time with the baffling, energetic, worrisome trio who called him Papa.

"I would never have suspected you of such kite-flying abilities," Miss Faraday said, linking her arm through Sedgemere's. "Your boys will brag about you for weeks."

All three, even Ralph, had bellowed their encouragement when Sedgemere had taken over from Ryland to rescue a kite flirting with captivity in the boughs of a pasture oak. Their cries of "Capital, Papa!" and "Papa, you did it!" should have been audible back in Nottinghamshire.

"They will brag about you, my dear," Sedgemere countered. "The known world expanded when they saw you skipping rocks."

Miss Faraday walked along with him companionably, her straw hat hanging down her back like any goose-girl on a summer day. Sedgemere had come to the astounding conclusion that Miss Faraday enjoyed touching him. Simply enjoyed touching him.

She hugged the boys—fleetingly, in deference to their dignity, but good, solid squeezes. She patted their heads, she took their hands, and she sat right next to them on benches and picnic blankets.

She linked arms with Sedgemere, took his hand, tidied his cravat, and even—he'd nearly fainted with disbelief—brushed a hand over his hair when the breeze had mussed it. She'd done so in the walled garden of The Duke's Arms, but that very morning, she'd done the same thing within sight of all three boys.

And that too, had apparently fascinated Sedgemere's progeny.

"I was skipping rocks before I could write my name," Miss Faraday said. "My father wanted sons, of course. What man doesn't? But he got me. He calls me a great, healthy exponent of the winsome gender, and made do with me as best he could."

Hannibal Faraday was a shrewd, cheerful soul, but what was wrong with the banker, that he couldn't treasure the daughter he'd been given? Anne was lovely, practical, kind, and indifferent to the typical insecurities and machinations of single young women.

"So your papa taught you to skip rocks?" Sedgemere asked. They were strolling around Veramoor's ornamental lake, the hour being too early for the other guests to be out of bed, and too late for rambunctious boys to remain imprisoned in the nursery.

"My papa taught me to skip rocks," Miss Faraday said, as the path wended into the trees bordering the lake. "Also to shoot, to ride astride—my mother intervened when I was eight—and generally gave me a gentleman's education."

How... lonely, for a young girl. How isolating. "The term gentleman's education is a contradiction in terms," Sedgemere observed. "Young boys go off to school to learn bullying, gossiping, flatulence, and drinking. Had it not been for Hardcastle—"

"Well done, Richard!" Miss Faraday yelled. "I counted four bounces!"

Sedgemere had used the word flatulence in the presence of a lady. A gentleman, regardless of what passed for his education, ought not to do that.

"Well done!" Sedgemere called. "Excellent momentum!"

"Papa says you have a good arm," Ryland shouted.

Richard saluted, grinning, then squatted along the lakeshore, likely searching for another rock. Ralph was tempting the ducks closer to the bank with toast pilfered from a breakfast tray, and Ryland threw sticks as far out into the lake as he could.

"You are such a good papa," Miss Faraday said. "The boys will recall this house party for the rest of their lives, and they'll remember these mornings with you."

Sedgemere would recall these mornings for the rest of his life. As much as he wanted to kiss Anne Faraday again, he'd mustered his patience the better to study her. What single woman of common birth disdained a ducal husband?

Why did Anne look skeptically upon him as a possible husband, when apparently, she found him physically appealing, enjoyed his company, and even enjoyed the company of his children?

As a result of his caution, Sedgemere had spent time with the lady apart from the other guests, and in the presence of the children. He still wanted very much to kiss her—at least to kiss her—but his attraction was growing roots and leaves, blossoming from respect into admiration, from liking into warmth.

He'd spoken of becoming better acquainted, but he'd envisioned becoming better acquainted with her kisses, with the feel of her hands in his hair. He'd not realized that watching her teach Ralph to skip rocks might also be part of the bargain.

"I am on to your tricks, madam," Sedgemere said. "You have the knack of finding something agreeable about the boys and praising them for it. They, who have perhaps two percent praiseworthy behaviors by natural inclination, double their efforts in benevolent directions, and thus their demeanor improves."

"It improves exponentially," she said. "My mother took the same approach with me, the servants, and, I suspect, Papa."

Exponentially was an interesting, academic, and appropriate term, also accurate when applied to the increase in Sedgemere's regard for Miss Faraday. He patted her bare hand, kite-flying being a bare-handed undertaking.

"You take the same approach with me, madam." And it was working. The boys had been so much troublesome baggage when Sedgemere had arrived. Now this hour with them was the most enjoyable of the day. He'd learned to notice and enjoy his own sons.

Better still, his boys were enjoying their papa. Ralph had gone so far as to snatch Sedgemere by the hand and drag him to the lakeshore for Miss Faraday's rock-skipping demonstration.

"I think you should round up the other children in the nursery and challenge them to a raft-building contest," Miss Faraday said, as she accompanied Sedgemere deeper into the trees. "The lake isn't three feet deep at the center, and the weather is obligingly hot."

The lake was five feet deep at the center, but only at the center. "Will you kiss me if I propose a raft-building contest to our host and hostess?"

"I will probably kiss you regardless," the lady replied. "If the adults undertake boat races, you must be sure to assign Mr. Willingham to the same boat as Miss Cunningham."

"Of course." Sedgemere would be equally sure to assign Miss Faraday to the boat *he* captained. "Do I take it you can swim, Miss Faraday?"

"Like a fish, though there isn't much call for swimming in the management of Papa's household. This shade feels divine. If we picnic later today, we must picnic near these trees."

Sedgemere had positive associations with picnics. Hardcastle would chaperone, of course, and any picnic was hours of bowing, chatting, and amiability away.

"Might I look forward to a kiss at this picnic, madam?"

"You may look forward to a kiss this very moment, Your Grace."

* * * * *

The lake had expanded the longer Anne had wandered its shore with Sedgemere. Once she and his grace reached the tree line, they'd be out of view of the house, the stable, the children, and out of reach of Anne's common sense and her conscience. The tree line, alas, seemed to recede with each step Anne took toward it, until she and her escort finally gained the cool privacy of the woods.

Sedgemere had played the pianoforte with casual competence when Miss Higgindorfer had needed an accompanist the previous evening. At dinner, he always sat well up the table from Anne and kept all the titled ladies tittering and smiling, though Anne had yet to see him smile.

And he'd made no move whatsoever to kiss Anne again.

They were wasting days, and nights, and Papa's letters already anticipated the happy moment when Anne would be back, *"where she belonged."*

Here was where Anne belonged, beside Sedgemere on a wooded path in the Whinlatter forest.

"I am to look forward to a kiss this very moment?" His Grace asked. "Or am I to enjoy a kiss this very moment?"

The air smelled different in the woods, earthier. The lakeshore was ferns and rocks right up to the water rather than the pebbled beach constructed closer to the house. Birds flitted overhead, and across the lake, a duck honked indignantly.

"You are waiting for me to kiss you?" Anne asked.

Sedgemere's hand trailed down her arm, a simple caress through the muslin of her sleeve.

"Matters seem to go well when we kiss each other, Miss Faraday." The duke bent his head as Anne leaned toward him, and the morning transformed from pretty to transcendent.

Anne had seen such a transition before, when a young lady of her acquaintance had been proposed to at a formal ball. The smitten gentleman had gone down on bended knee, flourished a big, sparkly ring, and made his intended the toast of the evening with his gallantry. The young lady had been transfigured for the evening, not merely pretty, but luminous.

And so the simple act of Sedgemere's lips brushing Anne's changed the day from a summer morning in the Lakes to a moment of heaven. He kept her hand in his, folded her fingers against his heart, and threaded his free hand into her hair.

"God, the taste of you," he muttered against her mouth. "The feel of you."

The feel of him, solid and familiar, but *terra incognita* too. Anne roamed Sedgemere with her hands, hungry to learn his contours. He was hard angles, solid muscle, and fine tailoring, until her explorations ventured from his shoulders and jaw to his hair.

His hair was warm, spun sunshine. The boys, being redheads, didn't have this silky, swan's-down hair. The duke's cravat was more frothy pleasure, sartorial exuberance in its exquisite blond lace edging and in the sheer abundance of fabric.

Sedgemere's tongue made entreaties against Anne's lips, and she let him have her weight, the better to focus on the intimacies he offered. He tasted of toothpowder and of the sprig of lavender he'd stuck between his lips when he'd crossed the garden.

Sedgemere shifted, and Anne's back was to a sturdy tree. The squirrels and birds had gone quiet. The water lapped rhythmically against the rocks, in time with the desire beating through Anne's veins.

"The boys—" Sedgemere said, bracing a forearm near Anne's head.

"I want—" Rather than waste time with words, Anne showed him what she wanted: him, snug against her, the evidence of his arousal a reassuring reality against her belly. She hooked a leg around his thigh and got a fistful of his hair.

This was not a tame, unplanned garden kiss. This was a kiss she'd anticipated for days and nights, a kiss that could lead to wicked pleasures and glowing memories.

Sedgemere's mouth cruised down Anne's throat, the sensation maddeningly tender, then he changed direction, nuzzling a spot beneath her ear that conjured heat in her middle. Anne clutched his shoulders, lest her knees buckle, or her fingers busy themselves unfastening his clothing.

When she found Sedgemere's mouth, she offered him a kiss of wanton, reckless desire, for a taste of Sedgemere was a treat both luscious and bitter. She could not have him. She could only sample him, and the sheer fury of that frustration gave her desire a desperate edge.

"Papa! I found a frog!"

Ralph's voice. Anne had found a handsome prince, but she must throw him back.

"He found a toad!" Ryland, ever the knowledgeable older brother.

"Anne, love, you mustn't be upset," Sedgemere whispered, kissing her brow. His thumb traced the side of her face, his breath whispered across her cheek. "Plead an indisposition tonight, and I'll come for you."

She managed a nod. Sedgemere straightened, and a shaft of sunlight smacked her in the eyes. She let him go when she wanted to grab his hand and disappear with him into the forest for the next hundred years.

By the time the boys came pelting into the woods, Anne had jammed her straw hat onto her head and slapped a smile on her face. She even admired the toad, a grand warty creature whom the boys named Wellington.

And then she made them turn him loose, because a duke, even an amphibian duke, must be allowed to go about his business, as Sedgemere would go about his when the house party ended.

* * * * *

"If you look at the clock one more time," Hardcastle muttered as he took the chair beside Sedgemere, "the entire assemblage will know an assignation awaits you."

Miranda Postlethwaite, sister to the shorn poodle of long ago, barely hid her frustration at Hardcastle's choice of seat, for she'd apparently taken it into her head to become Sedgemere's duchess.

Across the room, the poor Higgindorfer woman commenced an aria about death being the only consolation when true love proved fickle. Her voice was lovely, though her accompanist was some clod-pated earl or other.

"I'm still fatigued from watching my sons ride Veramoor's sheep," Sedgemere whispered back. From laughing so hard his sides had nearly split. Even Ralph had been overcome with merriment, though Miss Faraday—instigator of the impromptu sheep races—had bellowed the loudest encouragement.

"You're fatigued from an excess of ridiculousness," Hardcastle mused. "One never would have guessed utter frivolity required stamina. Have you proposed to Miss Faraday yet? You're a hopeless nincompoop if you haven't. It's all very well to affix your boys to the backs of hapless ovines, and allow the children to charm the lady with their foolishness, but you won't find her like again, Sedgemere."

No, he would not. "For your information, I have the lady's permission to embark on a wooing."

Hardcastle crossed his legs, a gesture he alone managed to make elegant instead of fussy. "A wooing that involves sheep races. Subtle, Sedgemere. You'll start a new fashion at Almack's, I'm sure."

The wooing involved kisses too. In the woods along the lake and later in the day, behind the stable while scouting a proper course for the sheep races—not that the sheep viewed a racecourse as anything other than more space to graze.

"Are you jealous, Hardcastle?"

"Terribly. I've always wanted to throw a leg over a sheep and hang on for dear life while the crazed beast did its utmost to fling me into the dung heap."

Anne's observation about Hardcastle being shy came to mind. She'd described the upbringing of a young duke as dull and miserable, and she'd been right. The upbringing of a *shy* young duke would also be... lonely.

"You don't fancy any of the young ladies on offer, do you?" Sedgemere asked. "Miss Higgindorfer seems nice enough, and you'd have all the Italian opera you'd ever want."

"She fancies Willingham, and I do not fancy opera."

Hardcastle loved music. He'd been teased for it by the other boys at school and hadn't been heard to play the pianoforte since. Did the prodigy of a governess enjoy music? Could she play, even a little?

A glance at the clock revealed that four entire minutes had elapsed since Sedgemere had last checked the time.

"I thought Miss Cunningham had set her cap for Willingham," Sedgemere said. "One can see how Veramoor and his duchess would find such gatherings amusing. Rather like several chess games in progress at once."

"Propose to Miss Faraday, Sedgemere. Other fellows have remarked the warmth of her laughter, the affection she showers on the children."

Other fellows including... *Hardcastle?*

"I believe she is testing me, Hardcastle. She's been pursued by men of high degree, fellows whose intentions were not flattering to anybody. You're right that Anne is an heiress—her papa has mentioned specifics to me—and she's right to be skeptical of any man's advances."

"Anne. You refer to the lady by her first name. Hmm."

Polite applause followed, for true love had finally accepted its bitter fate and faded to a wilting descending cadence.

"You will make my excuses," Sedgemere said, rising. "Too much sun, the press of business, neglecting my correspondence, et cetera."

"Take care, Your Grace. *Amor et melle et felle est fecundissimus.*"

Love is rich with both honey and venom. "Pleasant dreams to you too, Hardcastle."

Sedgemere quit the music room without allowing a single lady to catch his eye, for Hardcastle's observation had been too close to the mark. Anne kissed with a fervor that delighted and intrigued, she was unstinting in her affection for the boys, and she showed every appearance of welcoming a dalliance from one of the most eligible bachelors in the realm.

She also disappeared to her room by the hour, pleading a need for rest, or to pen a letter to her distant papa. She avoided any topic that related to the future, and she disdained the notice of every eligible young man, attributing even courtesies solely to an interest in her father's wealth.

Not without justification, apparently, for her father was obscenely wealthy.

Sedgemere stopped by his rooms to make use of his toothpowder and change out of formal attire. When a gentleman bent on wooing intended to take his lady swimming, the fewer clothes, the better.

CHAPTER 5

The tap on Anne's door was expected. The conflict about whether to heed Sedgemere's summons was not.

Anne planned to dally with Sedgemere, then send him on his way. His Grace's intentions were honorable, and Anne dreaded the day when she saw disgust in his keen blue eyes.

She opened the door anyway. "Your Grace. Good evening."

The duke was in riding attire, though of course he wouldn't go riding when the hour was nearly midnight. Never had snug breeches, tall boots, and a billowing shirt beneath an embroidered waistcoat looked so attractive. He carried a hamper in one hand. His jacket was slung over his other arm.

"Madam, you are invited to a stroll by the lake. I'd bow, but that would look silly with my present encumbrances."

"Can't have you looking silly," Anne said, snatching a shawl and joining him in the corridor. "I was half expecting you to have a go at riding Veramoor's ram earlier today."

"Your hair is down," Sedgemere said. "I've never seen your hair down."

Anne's hair was tidily braided. "Nobody save my lady's maid has seen my hair *down*, Your Grace. Are we in a footrace?"

"Nobody?" Sedgemere paused with one hand on the doorway to the servants' stairs. "I would like to be the first, then. Also the last."

He went bounding down the stairs, leaving Anne to follow at a more decorous pace. Sedgemere still hadn't precisely proposed, which was fortunate. For when he proposed, she'd have to refuse him.

They emerged on the side of the house that faced the lake, away from the thumping of the pianoforte, away from lights and applause and curious eyes. The water reflected the silvery moonshine, a slight breeze riffled the surface.

"I've been reconnoitering all day," Sedgemere said, striding off, "looking for the perfect spot: Close to the house, for the less time spent hiking in the dark, the better. Far enough away from the house that nobody would hear us talking if they left a window up. Near the lake, because the lake is beautiful, but tucked beneath the trees, because privacy is of utmost concern. Then too—"

Anne hauled him up short by virtue of yanking on the handle of the hamper he carried. She took the hamper from him, draped his jacket over it, then stepped into his arms.

"I've missed you, Sedgemere. All through dinner—"

Through every moment. When he'd roared with laughter at the boys on their wooly steeds, when he'd picked Ralph up and tossed him into the air as the victor, when he'd sauntered into the blue gallery in his evening attire. Anne could not lay eyes on Sedgemere without her heart aching.

She'd accosted him beneath one of the many oaks that dotted Veramoor's lawn. They would not be visible from the house, so she indulged in the need to kiss him.

Sedgemere obliged with delicate, patient, maddening return fire, until Anne's thigh was wedged between his legs, and she was clinging to him simply to remain upright.

"About that perfect spot," Sedgemere said.

Anne leaned into him, his heartbeat palpable beneath her cheek. When she was with him, her awareness of the natural world was closer to the surface. The breeze swaying through the boughs of the oak, the water lapping at the shore, the rhythm of Sedgemere's life force, all resonated with the desire raging through Anne for the man in her arms.

"No spot can be perfect," Anne said, and all house parties came to an end.

"Your kisses are perfect," he said. "Shall we sit for a moment and pretend to admire the moon?" Sedgemere withdrew a blanket from the hamper, and Anne grabbed one edge of a quilt worn soft with age.

The quilt bore the scent of cedar, a good blanket for making memories on. Sedgemere backed up a few steps, so the frayed edge of the fabric lay directly at the foot of the oak. The shadows here were deep, while the forest rose in a great, black mass behind the lake. Above it, stars had been scattered across the firmament by a generous hand.

"If I proposed tonight, would you decline my suit?" Sedgemere asked.

"I admire persistence," Anne said, folding down onto the blanket. "I'm no great fan of badgering."

Sedgemere ought to have flounced back into the house. He instead came down beside Anne, undid his waistcoat, and tugged off his boots.

"You're stubborn," he said. "Stubborn is a fine quality. You're also not wearing stays."

"I expected we'd go swimming," Anne said.

He arranged his boots, waistcoat, and stockings at the edge of the blanket.

"So did I, but have you any idea, madam, any notion, what the image of you in a wet chemise does to my thought processes?"

As a result of that last embrace, Anne had some idea what such an image did to his breeding organs.

"Probably the same thing the image of you naked to the waist in sopping wet breeches does to mine, Your Grace. The water would be warm too, because the lake is shallow and the sun has been fierce."

In the next instant, Anne was on her back, fifteen stone of half-dressed duke above her.

"The sun has been fierce, indeed. You made Ralph laugh, my dear. You made *me* laugh. I've every confidence you made the sheep laugh too."

Sedgemere's kisses bore no laughter. They were all dark wine, billowing wind, and honeysuckle moon shadows.

Anne wiggled, she squirmed, she yanked on the duke's hair and shoved at him, until Sedgemere was lying between her legs, his weight a necessary but insufficient complement to the desire rioting through her.

"You needn't be noble," Anne panted between kisses. "I'm not a virgin, though once upon a time, I was a fool."

She took a risk, telling him that, but Sedgemere didn't pull away. Instead, he shifted up, so Anne could hide her flaming face against his throat. His hand cradled the back of her head, and he pressed his cheek to her temple.

"I'm sorry," he said, his grip fierce and cherishing. "Whoever he was, he was not worthy of your regard, and you are well rid of him. We'll speak of it if you like. I'll ruin him for you, I'll even kill him, but please, my love, not now."

My love. Anne could be Sedgemere's love, for a span of days. She wrapped herself around him, yearning and frustration turning the cool evening hot.

"I want you," she said, trying to get her hands on his falls. "Sedgemere, I'm tired of waiting, of being patient. We have only days, and I can't stand the thought that—"

The duke reared back and pulled his shirt over his head. In the moonlight, he was cool curves and smooth muscles. Anne wanted to nibble on his shoulders, and lick his ribs, and—

He stood, peeling his breeches off and kicking them to the grass, so the entire, magnificent naked whole of him stood before her.

"My name is Elias," he said. "Given my state of undress, I invite you, and you alone of all women, to call me by my name."

He wanted to give her his name, in other words. Anne could accept only part of his proffer.

"Elias, I'll need help with my chemise." Not because she couldn't reach the bows. Anne had chosen her attire for this outing carefully. She needed her lover's help because her hands shook too badly.

His, by contrast, were competent and brisk, untying each bow in succession, until Anne's chemise was undone, her treasures guarded only by Sedgemere's consideration and her own lack of courage.

"Leave it on if you like," he said, kissing Anne onto her back. "I don't need to see you to know that you're glorious."

He was glorious, finding the exact right balance between haste and leisure, between boldness and delicacy. With maddening gentleness, he caressed Anne's breasts through the cotton of her chemise, until she was the one to shove the fabric aside and arch into his hands.

She loved that he'd be naked with her, loved that every inch of him was available for her delectation. Memories, of clothing shoved aside while somebody slogged through an endless Schubert sonata on the next floor down, tried to intrude.

Anne figuratively threw those memories in the lake. Sedgemere was not a presuming earl, trying to get his hands on her dowry by virtue of hastily fumbling beneath her skirts. Sedgemere was, in fact, in no hurry whatsoever, for which Anne was tempted to kill him.

She bit his earlobe. "If you do not apply yourself to the task at hand with more focus, Your Grace, I will toss you into the water."

He glowered down at her, his hair tousled, his chest pressing against her breasts with each breath.

"Call me Elias, by God. You'll not be Your-Gracing me when I'm inside your very body, woman."

Anne lifted her hips against him. "Your Grace, Your Grace, Your Gr—oh, *my*."

His aim was excellent, his self-restraint pure torment. Slowly, by teasing advances and retreats, Sedgemere joined their bodies, while Anne's grasp of words, intentions, everything but Sedgemere unraveled.

"Say my name," he growled, bracing himself on his forearms.

He could keep up this rhythm all night, Anne suspected. All summer. For the rest of eternity. Her mind knew he expected some response from her, words of some sort. The rest of her was incoherent with relief to have him inside her, and with yearning for yet more of him.

She ran her foot up his flank, then locked her ankles at the small of his back. The ground was hard beneath her back, and that was good, because she needed the purchase to push into Sedgemere's thrusts, to love him back.

"Say my name, Anne."

She tried to harry him, to say what she needed with her body. "Sedgemere, *please*."

He kissed her, a quick smack when she wanted to devour his mouth. "Good try, but you'll have to do better, my dear."

Perhaps to inspire her, he sped up for the space of five breath-stealing thrusts, then returned to a slower tempo.

"Dammit, *Elias.*"

He laughed and showed her how much he'd been holding back. The starry sky reflected Anne's pleasure, in fiery streaks of desire and surprise, and then more and more pleasure, as if the entire lake had left its bounds to deluge her in sweet, sweet satisfaction. Cool fire and moonlit water, then the solid comfort of the earth beneath her, and the lovely stirring of a breeze over her heated skin.

Sedgemere gave her long moments to simply glory in the experience, and to recover. Anne stroked his hair, kissed his shoulder, and wished she had words instead of fleeting caresses to offer him.

Then he moved again inside her lazily, teasing her into another brief, blinding moment of gratification that helped Anne hold back the regret stalking her joy. When he kissed her temple, then gathered her close and simply held her, she yet managed to savor the sheer pleasure, and keep the tears at bay.

When Sedgemere withdrew, however, and spilled his seed on her belly, she told herself his consideration was for the best, even while she wept.

* * * * *

Sedgemere braced himself on one elbow, the effort of withdrawing from his lover having resulted in a combination of relief—he'd done the impossible in tearing himself from her, after all—and rage. Everything in him rebelled at his caution. His body had spent itself in a confused torrent of pleasure and dismay, his mind refused to function, and even the natural wariness of the wealthy, powerful duke was looking on in bewildered disbelief.

What would Anne think of him, nearly proposing one instant, then protecting his freedom in the next?

Fortunately, his gentlemanly honor had maintained the upper hand, for Anne's freedom had been protected as well.

She passed him a handkerchief.

"You do this part," she said, her hand falling to the blanket in languid surrender. "I can't move."

"I can't think," Sedgemere muttered, wiping the evidence of his passion from her pale midriff. "God above, Anne Faraday."

Should he propose again now? Hold her? Leave her in peace? Being a duke did not prepare a man for being a lover, much less a fiancé on offer.

"We ought to go for a swim," Anne said. "Though we might set the lake aboil."

Her voice was different, not so crisp, not so... confident.

"You aren't going anywhere, madam," Sedgemere said, finishing with the handkerchief and tossing it in the direction of his boots. He'd wash that handkerchief himself and treasure it all his days. "I will expire if you abandon me for the pleasures of a brisk swim, for any pleasures save those available in my embrace."

Anne rolled to her side, giving him her back. "You would have to carry me to the lake, Elias. Even a dozen steps are beyond me. What a formidable lover you are."

Elias. Freely given, affectionately rendered. The last of the frustration resulting from their truncated joining slipped away. Sedgemere tucked himself around his lady and flipped the quilt over them.

"When I think of the days I've wasted flying kites and skipping rocks," he said, nuzzling her nape. "Stewarding sheep races, for pity's sake."

"Every duke needs a talent to fall back on when the title pales," Anne replied, kissing his forearm. "You will be the foremost steward in all the realm for sheep races."

Anne had explained to the boys how to jockey a sheep, waved her hat madly to inspire the sheep to complete the racecourse, and hoisted Ralph into Sedgemere's arms at the conclusion of the contest. From there, Sedgemere had naturally put the boy on his shoulders and lost the last remaining bit of his heart into Anne Faraday's keeping.

Her inherent kindness extended even to taking care of male hopes and dreams, to nurturing the tender male ego.

"Stewarding sheep races is indeed a demanding and much sought-after profession," Sedgemere said. "Might I also aspire to become the steward of your heart, Anne?"

Her posture remained the same, sprawled on her side, her bum tucked into the lee of Sedgemere's body, her cheek pillowed on his biceps, her feet tucked between his calves.

The moment changed, nonetheless, and Sedgemere wasn't quite sure how. Did that stillness mean he had her full attention, or that she was poised to march off into the night?

"You already have my heart, Sedgemere. You had it the moment you noticed that Helen Trimble regards me as if I were the evidence of a passing goose on the bottom of her shoe. You had it when you lent me your teams all the way up from Nottinghamshire. You had it when I saw how protective you are of Hardcastle, though he hardly needs protecting. You had it when you realized your boys are in want of encouragement."

Sedgemere was encouraged, for this litany had nothing to do with his title, or with his consequence. He'd merely behaved as a gentleman toward... well, as a besotted gentleman.

"You imply that my lovemaking did not impress you," he said, his hand finding its way to a warm, abundant breast. "Shall I address that shortcoming?"

She lifted her cheek from his arm. "Somebody has lit the lamps in the nursery."

Against Sedgemere's palm, flesh ruched delicately. "One of the boys had a nightmare or started a pillow fight."

He'd like to have pillow fights with Anne, also formal dinners, house parties, holidays, quiet breakfasts, afternoon naps…

And babies.

"Sedgemere, your boys have that bedroom just before the corner. Why would they be awake at this hour?"

"They should be cast away with their labors, you've kept them so active," Sedgemere said, withdrawing his hand. "I suppose you want to investigate?"

Anne scrambled to sitting, and gathered up her chemise. "What if one of the boys has fallen ill? Feeding a great herd of people can mean the kitchen is less careful to keep hot food hot and cold food cold. Bad fish can carry a grown man off, or bad eggs. Mutton can turn, and if the sauces are heavy, and a boy is hungry, he might not notice."

Oh, how Sedgemere loved her, loved her fierce protectiveness of the boys, her ferocious passion, her laughter.

Her hesitance to accept his offer of marriage was not so endearing.

"Anne, calm yourself. They are robust boys, and nobody in the entire gathering has shown a single symptom of ill health. They know not to eat anything that tastes off, because a duke's heir might be drugged and kidnapped."

Her head emerged from her chemise. "Gracious, Sedgemere, you lead an exciting life. Hadn't you best get dressed?"

He did not want to get dressed. He wanted to tackle Anne and ravish her and tickle her, and then make love with her in the warm, shallow waters of the lake.

"Anne, will you marry me?"

"Now is not the time, Sedgemere. Your children might be ill, fevered, dyspeptic. One of them might be injured, or might have gone missing. One must always be aware of risks, and with children, the risks are limitless."

Not a *yes*, but also not a *no*, and she was right. Now was not the time. Sedgemere found his shirt, then pulled on his breeches.

"It's probably nothing. Ralph still occasionally wet the bed as recently as last summer. His brothers helped him hide the sheets and get new ones from the linen closet. I wouldn't have known if I hadn't overheard the housemaids discussing it."

The dress went on next, a loose, high-waisted smock with short sleeves and a lace-edged bodice. Of all Anne's dresses, including her dinner finery and ballroom attire, this one would always be Sedgemere's favorite.

"You should be proud of the boys for sticking together," she said. "Not all brothers do. I can't find my—"

Sedgemere passed her a pair of low-heeled slippers. "I am proud of the boys, and lately, I've started telling them that. I do hope Ralph hasn't wet the bed. He'll be mortified."

"Perhaps his duck has got loose," Anne said, kneeling up to help Sedgemere with his cravat. "Any duck would grow restless, living in boxes and closets."

"His *what?*"

"Josephine, his duck. I come out before breakfast for a walk around the lake, and Ralph is often in company with Josephine, whom he has brought clear from Nottinghamshire. She's a very well-traveled duck. Hold still, Sedgemere."

Anne finger-brushed his hair into order, fluffed his cravat, and passed him his jacket.

Because she was studying him, Sedgemere had a moment to study her. The moon had risen higher, and thus more light was available, and he could see what she doubtless hoped was hidden by the darkness.

Despite her brisk tone, despite her obvious concern for the children—and this damned traveling duck— Sedgemere's intimate attentions had moved Anne Faraday to tears.

Now was not the time, she'd said, but as Sedgemere took her hand and led her back to the house, he vowed that they would find the time, and he'd have an answer to why his lovemaking had made her cry.

And an answer to his proposal of marriage.

* * * * *

The maids were in an uproar, Richard and Ryland were pacing about in their nightshirts, a footman hovered, and two governesses in nightcaps and night-robes were arguing about whose job it was to evict rogue ducks.

Sedgemere stood in the middle of this pandemonium as if nursery riots were simply another duty on the endless list of duties dukes took in stride, while Anne could not find a useful thought to think or a helpful deed to do. Three older boys from the room across the corridor lingered in the doorway, and a small red-haired girl peeked around the jamb as well.

"The lot of you will please settle down." Sedgemere hadn't raised his voice, and he'd hoisted Ralph onto his hip. "Lord Ralph, when did you last see the duck?"

"She was in her b-box after supper," Ralph wailed, "but somebody let her out. I'll never s-see her again, and Josie was my only d-duck."

Two of the boys hovering in the door slipped away, the footman took to bouncing forward and back on his toes, and everybody else fell silent.

"You," Sedgemere said to the footman, "please follow the two fellows who departed and search their quarters. If you require my aid in that endeavor, I'll happily lend it, and I'm sure the boys' parents will too. You two," he went on, addressing the governesses, "are excused with my apologies for the uproar. If you maids would see the other children to their beds and search the playrooms for any stray ducks, I'd appreciate it."

"But my Josephine is lost," Ralph moaned. "My only d-duck, and she won't know her way around, and the other boys are mean, and the cook will kill her and feed her to the guests."

"Anne," Sedgemere said, "in the morning, you'll have a word with the

Duchess of Veramoor if Josephine remains truant. Please instruct Her Grace to modify the menus so no duck is served until Josephine has been returned to her owner's care."

One did not instruct the Duchess of Veramoor, but that wasn't the point. "Certainly, Sedgemere. I'll speak with Her Grace before breakfast."

"Can you do it tonight?" Ralph asked. Tears streaked his pale cheeks, and he didn't even raise his head from his papa's shoulder.

"Morning will suffice," Sedgemere said. "Nobody is awake in the kitchen to wield so much as a butter knife at this hour, my boy, and duck is never served for breakfast. It isn't done."

A great sigh went out of the child as Sedgemere sat on the edge of a low cot, arranging Ralph in his lap.

"You lot," he said, gesturing to Ryland and Richard. "Get over here. We have a mystery to solve. Miss Faraday, your powers of deduction are required in aid of our task."

Anne took a seat on the opposite cot, because Ryland and Richard had tucked in on each side of their papa. The picture they made, three handsome little redheads clustered around their blond papa, all serious focus on a missing duck, did queer things to Anne's heart.

She had no powers of deduction, but her predicament didn't call for any. She was not simply attracted to Sedgemere, she loved him. This slightly tousled fellow was the true man, not the wealthy aristocrat, but the conscientious parent, Hardcastle's devoted friend, Anne's lover—her wooer. Sedgemere's passion was a sumptuous pleasure Anne would never forget, but the devotion to his children, to finding a missing duck, would hold her heart captive forever.

"Now," Sedgemere said. "We've cleared the room of spies and spectators. If you wanted to hide a duck somewhere that would cause a great commotion and embroil the duck's owner in terrible trouble, where would you boys stash the duck?"

"Not in my rooms," Richard said. "Maybe in the governess's rooms?"

"The governesses would be shrieking the house down by now," Ryland observed. "Josie's not the quietest duck."

"We have to find her," Ralph said. His hand came up, thumb extended as if headed for his mouth, but Sedgemere gently trapped Ralph's hand in his own.

"Miss Faraday," Sedgemere said, "where would an errant duck cause the staff or guests the greatest disruption? Where would a duck be the worst possible surprise?"

Four sets of blue eyes turned on Anne as if she knew the secret to eternal happiness and how to remove an ink stain from a boy's favorite shirt. If she failed them—

"The linen closet on the floor that houses the young ladies," Anne said, rising. "I know exactly where it is too, because it's around the corner from my own rooms."

"You fellows stay here," Sedgemere said, depositing Ralph on the bed. "If Josie should come waddling home, she'll be upset, and only Ralph will be able to catch her. We'll report back shortly. Miss Faraday, lead on."

Sedgemere extended a hand, and Anne took it. She ought not to have, not in front of the boys, not without an adult chaperone. But all too soon, she'd have to tell Sedgemere they could never be married, and so she took what she could, and clasped his hand.

CHAPTER 6

"A damned duck," Sedgemere groused, though he wanted to howl with laughter. "A damned duck has attached itself to my nursery retinue and I had no idea. A damned female duck."

"Josephine sounds like a boy to me," Anne said. "The lady ducks have the louder, more raucous voices, rather like debutantes."

Anne's voice was soft, tired, and determined, and her grip on Sedgemere's hand secure. He could hunt ducks with her all night, all year, for the rest of his natural days. Voices came from around the corner, and Sedgemere pulled Anne into an alcove inhabited by a pair of Roman busts.

Miss Higgindorfer and Miss Postlethwaite went giggling past, extoling the virtues of *His Grace's* manly physique and lovely dark hair.

"Poor Hardcastle," Sedgemere whispered. "You check the corridor."

Anne did, her stealth worthy of Wellington's pickets. She gestured Sedgemere out of hiding, but he first tugged her back into the alcove and stole a kiss.

"For luck," he said. "My son's happiness and his entire regard for his papa rest upon locating this prodigal duck."

"The linen closet is just down here," Anne said.

And the damned closet, as it turned out, was locked. "Boys can't get into a locked closet, and I doubt—"

A soft, plaintiff quack sounded from the other side of the door. Anne's lips quirked as she fished at the base of her braid and produced a hairpin.

"One carries extras," she said, "in case another lady might have need, or a duck might be trapped behind a locked door." She applied the hairpin to the lock, and the latch lifted easily.

They couldn't leave the door open, lest the duck fly off, so Sedgemere wedged himself through the door and towed Anne in after him.

"Gracious, it's quite dark," she said.

Sedgemere looped his arms around her. "And the blasted duck has gone quiet, but we did find her, so perhaps another kiss for luck will produce complete victory."

He had not the first inkling how to find a duck in a tiny, pitch-dark room, but finding Anne's mouth with his own involved no effort at all, only pleasure. He kissed her and kissed her and kissed her, until her back was against the shelves of sheets, towels, and bedclothes, and the scents of lavender and laundry starch had become Sedgemere's favorite aphrodisiacs.

He was on the point of opening his falls when a soft quack sounded near his left boot.

Anne's sigh feathered past his cheek. "I told you I think he's a boy duck. He just sniffed at my ankle."

"There'll be none of that," Sedgemere said, stooping to pick up the duck. "The only fellow who'll be sniffing at your ankles is me, madam. This is not a small duck."

The bird snuggled into Sedgemere's grasp as if weary of being at liberty. Sedgemere, however, was not weary of kissing Anne, so he leaned in for more, kissing her around the duck.

"We should go," Anne whispered, her hand framing Sedgemere's jaw. "It's late, and the boys will worry."

"We should be married," Sedgemere said, as Josephine quacked her—or his—agreement. "Even the duck agrees."

"I cannot marry you, Your Grace." She kissed him lingeringly. "I am needed in my father's house, and you should marry a woman of some consequence."

The duck quacked again, not as softly.

"Do you think I'm after your money?" Sedgemere asked. "I have no need of it, Anne. I need only you. The boys love you, you will make a fine duchess, and I—"

The door opened as the Duchess of Veramoor's crisp voice rang out. "I knew I heard something quacking. It appears, though, that we've found ourselves a duck and a duke—among others. I must say, this is most irregular. I do not recall a duck on my guest list."

* * * * *

Anne ended up holding the duck, stroking her fingers over Josephine's soft, smooth feathers, while the Duchess of Veramoor paced the boundaries of a private sitting room.

"Sedgemere, you are found in a linen closet kissing the stuffing out of an unmarried woman of good birth, *at my house party*. A duck is no sort of chaperone, and I'll not be able to keep the Postlethwaite creature quiet."

For Miss Postlethwaite had been at Her Grace's elbow when the linen closet door had been opened. Josephine had honked a merry welcome, and Anne's future had been destroyed.

More destroyed, which was semantically impossible.

"I was in the act of making Miss Faraday an honorable offer," Sedgemere said. "She had yet to fully explain her response."

Anne had been on the verge of explaining her way right into His Grace's breeches. She cuddled the duck, who bore that indignity quietly. They'd both had a challenging evening, after all.

"Sedgemere, you do me great honor," Anne said, gaze fixed on Josephine's bill, "but I cannot marry you. I have explained that I'm needed at my father's side."

The duchess sat, so Sedgemere had room to pace. "You think I'm in want of coin," he said. "That's the only explanation I can fathom. You are confused by the events of the evening, and your normal common sense has deserted you. I do not care that much,"—he snapped his finger at Anne, and Josephine made as if to nip at him—"for your wealth."

If only it were that simple. "Sedgemere, I am old enough to know my own mind, and we would not suit."

A great, big, fat, quacking falsehood, that. Even the duchess looked impatient with Anne.

"We won't sort this out tonight," Her Grace said. "I will speak to the Postlethwaite girl tomorrow. A maid outside Miss Postlethwaite's door will ensure my guest does not roam before breakfast, but that's as much as I can do."

Sedgemere paused at the window and twitched back a lacy curtain. From this side of the house, he'd have a view of the moonlit lake.

"You might remind Miss Postlethwaite," Sedgemere said, "that if she speaks a word against Miss Faraday, nothing I could say or do would stop Hardcastle from offering Miss Postlethwaite and her entire set the cut direct."

Anne took heart from that observation, because Hardcastle would also cut anybody who spoke a word against Sedgemere.

"Do you love another, Miss Faraday?" the duchess asked.

What an appalling question. "I am not *in* love with anybody save Sedgemere."

Ah, God, a mistake. A mistake brought on by the lateness of the hour, forbidden passion, and stray ducks.

"Are you with child by another?" Her Grace's tone brooked no dissembling, but her gaze was kind. "Young ladies can be taken advantage of, and you are honorable enough not to put a cuckoo in the Sedgemere nest."

Sedgemere's gaze was stricken. He dropped to the sofa beside the duchess like a rock flung into the lake.

"*Anne?*"

"Sedgemere is the first man to turn my head in more than five years. I have not behaved well, and I do apologize for abusing your hospitality, but that is the extent of the situation. I'll leave in the morning, and you may put it about that I enticed the duke to a dalliance, for that is the truth."

Anne had no experience enticing anybody to do anything, though, so the truth was unlikely to be believed.

"Sedgemere, do not try to hector the woman into becoming your wife," the duchess said, getting to her feet. "Miss Faraday's mother was equally resolute once her mind was made up, else she would never have married Hannibal Faraday. No family wants to see a daughter married off to an impecunious banker, but Fenecia was smitten. Miss Faraday has her mother's pretty looks, I'm told she has her mama's aptitude for numbers, and apparently, she has her mother's independence too. Off to bed with you two—separate beds, if you please."

Her Grace swept out, a small, forceful woman, who hadn't been surprised or even disappointed to find lovers in her linen closet kissing over a stray duck. If Anne were ever, through some miracle, to become a duchess, she'd aspire to such savoir faire.

In the present situation, however, it was all she could do not to cry.

"Give me the damned duck," Sedgemere said, "and do not think to hare off in the morning, like a naughty schoolgirl. If you run, the Postlethwaite creature will set the dogs of gossip upon you, but her aspirations in Hardcastle's direction will keep her quiet for the duration of the gathering."

They had a small wrestling match over the duck, mostly because Anne wanted any excuse to brush hands with Sedgemere. She'd apparently achieved the goal of rejecting his suit. Now all that remained was to survive a few more days, enduring the fruits of her victory.

* * * * *

After escorting Miss Faraday around the lake, Hardcastle bowed the lady on her way. This involved ignoring the despairing glance she sent toward Hardcastle's oldest and dearest pain in the arse, for Sedgemere was on his full ducal dignity on the far side of the terrace. His Grace of Sedgemere's excuse for spying on Miss Faraday—this time—was that most pressing of errands, accompanying a duck on its constitutional.

"I know not which of you is the more pathetic," Hardcastle said, crossing the terrace. "The house party ends tomorrow, and you're reduced to taking the air with an anatine companion. Where is your courage, Sedgemere? Storm the castle walls, sing the die-away ballads beneath the lady's window, muster a bit of derring-do."

Hardcastle had been introduced nearly two weeks and an eternity of tedium ago to Josephine. She waddled about in the grass below the terrace and would likely be as glad as Hardcastle to quit the party.

"How is Anne?" Sedgemere asked.

"Miserable. The only topics about which I can inspire her to discourse are canal projects and housing developments." The lady was also willing to listen to anything, anything at all, related to Sedgemere. His upbringing, his antecedents, his impatience with foreign languages, which Hardcastle attempted to redress by constant references to Latin.

"Then she and I are both miserable," Sedgemere said, lowering himself to the top step, as if he were a small boy, willing to sit anywhere on a summer day, provided he sat *outside*. "The only hypothesis I've concocted is that Anne fears I'm seeking her hand to gain control of her dowry. This is patently false, of course, also insufficient to explain her behaviors."

Hardcastle's delicate ducal ears were not equal to hearing the details of those behaviors. He'd attempted a late-night stroll around the lake several evenings ago, and had had to change his route not far from the house.

"You might try asking Miss Faraday why she's refused a life basking in your cherishing regard," Hardcastle suggested. "At least on the topic of compound interest, she's blazingly articulate."

"Hardcastle, have you been at the brandy this early in the day? Anne is not a solicitor, to be bored with your talk of business."

Josephine quacked, flapped her wings, and went strutting across the grass in the direction of another duck who'd come wandering up from the lake.

"Anne is a banker's daughter," Hardcastle said. "Can you imagine what the dinner conversation with her dear papa is like? Prinny's debts, Devonshire's racing wagers, the latest gossip on 'Change?"

"She's humoring you, Hardcastle," Sedgemere snapped. "Tossing conversational lures that will tempt you away from your pettifogging Latin aphorisms. What are those ducks about?"

The other duck was craning its neck and flapping its wings. Josephine carried on like a fellow who wanted to cut in partway through a waltz but couldn't attract the dancers' notice.

"Miss Faraday was not humoring me, Sedgemere. She waxed eloquent about a gentleman's education including the basics of finance, for hers certainly did, and she made a strong case for allowing children from a young age to—"

A furious quacking commenced from under the tree as Sedgemere shot to his feet. "That's *it*. That's what she's afraid of. Hardcastle, watch that duck and bring her inside with you, or Ralph will have a fit of the vapors. By God, Hardcastle you have your moments."

Hardcastle rose more slowly. "Whatever are you going on about, Sedgemere? Perhaps you're having a fit of the vapors." For which his grace was long overdue, in Hardcastle's opinion.

"Ryland told me Anne had explained multiplication to him, when the boy's barely grasped addition and subtraction. He's keen for math, though, so I thought Anne had simply humored a boy's interests. Then there's *exponentially*, and her mama marrying an impecunious banker who's now a damned nabob. I must talk to the duchess."

"While I wrangle quarreling ducks."

"Hardcastle, I do worry about you. Those ducks are not quarreling, and we'll have to change Josephine's name to Joseph."

Hardcastle risked a glance beneath the tree. "One shudders at the company you've dragged me into, Sedgemere. This house party has turned into a debauch for ducks. Why I ever agreed to chaperone you here escapes my traumatized mind. Be about your wooing, and plan to quit this den of iniquity at first light."

* * * * *

"I love him," Anne said, "but Sedgemere's a duke. His duchess will be in the public eye, and Nottinghamshire is so very far from London, where Papa must bide."

"Your mama would not like to see you in this state," the Duchess of Veramoor said, passing Anne a plate of French chocolates. They were making Anne sick, these chocolates, but she could not stop eating them.

"Mama's the one who made me promise I'd look after Papa, no matter what." Chocolates deserved a cold glass of milk, or perhaps a tot of fine brandy, not a pot of tepid gunpowder. "I've kept my promise, but Papa shows no signs of retiring, and he can't exactly take on a partner or sell the banks."

Anne had hinted enough in recent years to know he wouldn't. Papa loved the idea of leaving his little girl a stinking fortune, as if a fortune ever sent a lady on a duck hunt in the middle of the night, or loved her witless beneath the Cumbrian moon.

A knock sounded on the door of Her Grace's private parlor. This was the same room where Anne had rejected Sedgemere's proposal, though by day, it was a cheery place. Sunshine poured in the west-facing windows, and beyond the windows, the green expanse of the forest marched up the hillside behind the lake.

The knock came again, louder.

"Enter," the duchess said.

Sedgemere sauntered in, breathtakingly handsome in his country gentleman's attire, not a blond hair out of place and not a hint of warmth about his demeanor. Anne wanted to throw the entire box of chocolates at him and leave in fit of weeping.

And she wanted to have his children.

"Sedgemere, do stop glowering," Her Grace said, thumping the place beside her on the settee. "Your timing is awful. Anne was about to explain to me why she's being so dunderheaded, but I suppose that explanation is better given to you."

To Anne's horror, the duchess rose, helping herself to a chocolate. "Your mother married for love, Anne Faraday. She would not want to see you trapped beneath a heap of money." Her Grace departed, patting Sedgemere's cheek and munching on her chocolate.

"Miss Faraday, will you object if I close the door?" Sedgemere asked.

They were alone and she was no longer *Anne* to him. "You can't close the door," she retorted. "Any passing gossip will note that I'm private with you, *again*, and then all of Hardcastle's attempts to quell the rumors will be for naught. Let's take a final walk around the lake."

"No more perishing perambulations around the lake, if you please. Hardcastle is at this moment presiding over a duck orgy, though a brush with debauchery will do the old boy good. We'll visit the stable."

A duck orgy? Had Anne's rejection cost Sedgemere his reason?

"Come along," Sedgemere said, pulling Anne to her feet. "We have much to discuss, such as your mendacity, and your lamentable tendency to protect the fellows who give their hearts into your keeping."

That comment made no sense, for Anne had been telling the absolute miserable truth: She loved Sedgemere, and she could not become his duchess. Not ever.

* * * * *

The puzzle pieces added up, so to speak, the longer Sedgemere rearranged them in his mind. Anne came along quietly as Sedgemere escorted her to the Veramoor horse palace—many tenant cottages were not so comfortable, even on Sedgemere's estates—and then beyond, to a winding path through the trees.

"If you need privacy to berate me," Anne said, "the stable would have sufficed, Your Grace."

"I would needlessly upset the livestock, did we tarry in the stable, though I do need privacy for what must be said."

"You're a duke, sir. You understand about duty, and your duty is to find a duchess who can look the part and dance the part. She must host your political dinners, endure court functions with you, socialize at the very highest levels, while I've merely been propositioned at the very highest levels, and— Sedgemere, stop."

She untangled her arm from his and stood in a slanting beam of light like some fairy creature who'd disappear if Sedgemere blinked.

"*I love you*," Sedgemere said quietly, though he wanted to bellow the words to every corner of the realm. "And because I love you, madam, you will do me the courtesy of granting me a fair hearing."

His words were intended to capture the lady's attention, but she turned away.

"Unfair, Your Grace. Mortally unfair." Her shoulders were rigid with emotion—also graceful and pale.

Sedgemere wanted to shake her by those elegant, sturdy shoulders. Instead he stepped closer and spoke close to her ear.

"Give me five minutes, Anne Faraday. If after five minutes, you never want to see me again, I will do my utmost to oblige you."

She turned abruptly and gave him such kisses as ought to have set the woods ablaze. Even when they'd made love, Anne hadn't surrendered herself into his embrace with quite this much abandon, this much desperation. She kissed Sedgemere as if she would, indeed, send him packing.

Which would not do. Sedgemere picked his lady up and carried her to a fallen tree, one at the perfect height for a passionate embrace. Anne hauled him closer by the lapels of his coat and spread her knees so Sedgemere could stand between them.

They needed to talk, to sort their future out, but what *they* needed must, for a few moments, yield to what *Anne* needed.

"Anne, we needn't rush," Sedgemere whispered as she started unbuttoning his falls.

"We have no more time," she retorted. "I will miss you until the day I die, but we still have these moments, and Sedgemere, you must not make me beg."

Anne's kisses rather prevented anybody from begging for anything, at least verbally, so Sedgemere pleaded his case with warm caresses to those shoulders he'd admired earlier, and soft murmurs of appreciation for the turn of her knee, the elegant curve of her throat.

"You expect me to make love with you here and now?" Sedgemere whispered before she finished with his falls. "In the forest primeval, not ten yards from—God save me."

Anne's hands went diving beneath layers of expensive Bond Street tailoring, her grip both careful and determined.

"I want you," she said. "If this is all I can have of you, then please oblige me."

"I'm not the condemned prisoner's last meal," Sedgemere said, frothing skirts and petticoats up around the lady's waist. "I'm your intended, and the man who loves you."

He settled the argument with one sure thrust—or at least silenced Anne's reply—and then desire took over, until the far branches of the fallen tree upon which Anne perched were swaying to the give and take of Sedgemere's passion.

With Anne so desperate and silent, Sedgemere's desire became driven by a need to relieve her fears for their future. He slowed the pace and gentled his kisses, until the quiet of the woods, the stillness of the lake became a part of his lovemaking.

"I do love you," he said. "I will always love you."

"Elias, you must not—" Anne didn't finish that thought, which was prudent of her, because Sedgemere *would*, all afternoon if necessary. He'd caress her lovely breasts, kiss her beautiful shoulders, and silence her remonstrations with pleasure.

She allowed him enough time that his thighs eventually burned, the discomfort a small testament to a lover's devotion, and then his heart ached, when Anne seized the initiative and surrendered to satisfaction.

"You think I'll leave you now?" he said, stroking a hand over her hair. "You think I'll withdraw and abandon you, because your place is running your father's households as a dutiful spinster daughter?"

"You must," she said, though her arms remained lashed about his waist. "Tomorrow morning, Elias, you must return to Nottinghamshire, and I'll away to York."

Tonight, he'd announce their engagement, but first, Sedgemere undertook to give his lady the rest of the pleasure due her. He let his love for her fly free, let it show in every caress and thrust and kiss and moan, until Anne was again clinging to him, and whispering his name. He held off long enough to be sure she'd found satisfaction, and then he joined her in that place where nothing— not duty, not time, not fear or even worry—could crowd past the love he shared with her.

* * * * *

Love and hate were not opposites, they were... close cousins, for the more Anne loved Sedgemere, the more she hated what her life had become.

A fortune in lies and deceptions, a wearying farce that had no end. She loved her papa, of course, and she understood that a banker had obligations, a sacred duty based on trust. Far more depended on the trust placed in Papa than Anne's mere happiness.

A bank's good health could uphold that of a nation or a monarchy. A bank failing could be the ruin of many innocent lives. Her mother had taught her that almost before Anne could stitch a straight seam.

"Your bottom cannot be comfortable," Sedgemere said, scooping Anne off the tree trunk and setting her on her feet. "The rest of you is woefully unmussed."

Her mind was mussed. In moments, Sedgemere was buttoned up, his shirt tails tucked in, every evidence of their recent lovemaking gone, while Anne...

"I need your handkerchief, Your Grace."

A square of white linen appeared on Sedgemere's palm, held out to Anne as if on a tray. "So you do."

She didn't bother turning her back, but reached under her skirts and made use of the handkerchief, while Sedgemere hiked himself to sit on the fallen tree, an oak, from the looks of the wilting leaves.

"I'll take that," Sedgemere said, when Anne had finished.

He was so matter-of-fact about such earthy intimacies. Anne would not have predicted this about him, any more than she would have predicted his abilities as a steward of sheep races.

"I'll miss you," she said, folding the cloth carefully to hide evidence of its use. "I'll miss the boys too, but I think Hardcastle has been largely effective quelling any gossip about our kiss in the linen closet."

"You were right, you know," Sedgemere replied, tucking the handkerchief into a jacket pocket. "Josephine is a drake. You're also quite wrong, about missing me. You will have little occasion to miss me, when we're married. You might, however, miss very much being the brains behind your papa's vast financial empire. As your husband, I'll see that you remain at the helm of his fortune to the extent that's where you'd like to be."

* * * * *

Sedgemere cursed himself for a henwit when Anne silently braced herself against the tree trunk, as if she'd been informed of a great loss. He slid to his feet and pulled her into his embrace rather than risk her leaving him alone in the forest.

"Your mother had the same gift, I'd guess," he said. "It is a gift, you know, to be able to grasp finances, to see possibilities where others see only boring figures and limitations."

She was light in his arms, no more leaning on him than a beam of sunshine would lean on a breeze.

"From a young age," Sedgemere went on, "probably before your mama died, you've carried the burden of your father's banking enterprises on your own shoulders. You've chosen the investments, the projects, the risks, while he's gossiped at the clubs and signed the documents."

She shook her head, a curl coming loose from her bun. "You must not say such things. Papa is the banker. His grandfather started the bank, and Papa knows every customer, every account, every balance."

"But he doesn't grasp *money*," Sedgemere said. "He was struggling badly when your mother took him in hand, and he'd have lost several fortunes by now if you hadn't kept him from unwise investments. You read the papers voraciously, you correspond with him several times a day, and you've advised Hardcastle on his finances without His Grace even realizing it."

Anne began to shake, like a fading leaf in a strong autumn wind. "Sedgemere, you cannot believe that I, a mere spinster daughter, could hold the reins to some of the greatest fortunes in the realm. I manage the household, I deal with squabbling housemaids. I don't even know the names on many of the accounts."

Sedgemere tucked that stray curl back in its place when he wanted to undo her coiffure entirely.

"You make it a point not to know the names, to insist your father speak to you in hypotheticals and exercise what discretion he can. Nonetheless, the bank and all its titled, arrogant clients rely on you to increase the wealth in its coffers. That's what the flock of pigeons and platoon of special messengers are about. That's why you can explain multiplication to a boy who disliked addition and subtraction. That's why you will marry me."

She tore from his embrace and stomped off, deeper into the woods. "Don't you see, Sedgemere, Papa will fail without me. He nearly failed when Mama died, but she'd warned me I'd have to step in. He was about to invest in tulips—

tulips, of all the cautionary tales!—and I could not keep silent. Once he realized that I was as capable as Mama had been, he expected that I'd sort matters out."

"And you've been sorting them ever since," Sedgemere said, resisting the urge to haul her back into his arms. "You've done so well that his business has grown *exponentially*, and now you dare not take your hand off the tiller for even a few weeks."

She swung around to face him and crossed her arms, a feminine citadel of exasperation. "Not even for a few days. Papa takes odd notions and gets ahead of himself, and while I would love to be your wife, Sedgemere, I cannot have the fate of royal dukes and presuming earls on my hands. Papa could ruin them, especially now when they all trust him to produce such excellent returns. The Postlethwaites were courting ruin until two years ago. The Cheshires cannot afford another Season for both daughters. You see my predicament."

Sedgemere saw her brilliance, her frustration, her predicament, and her honor.

He also saw his future duchess. "My love, you have needed a partner. Your father was sensible enough to accept your help when it was offered. Will you be as wise? All that's wanted is a duke at your beck and call, a fellow somewhat wanting for charm, but well-endowed with consequence and devoted to you."

He took another step closer, for he had her attention. "I'll simply tell your dear papa that he's to dine with us once a week without fail, and that he's to hire the manager of your choosing, who will report to you. Hannibal will not sign a document without your permission, will not commit to an investment unless you've discussed it with him. I will further bruit it about that the ducal finances, including your dower funds, will be entrusted to his bank for safekeeping."

As Sedgemere stalked closer, Anne unfolded her arms. "You'd have me manage my own fortune?"

"Mine too, if you have time. I'll be too busy loving my wife and creating trouble in the Lords. Or keeping kites from disappearing into trees, stewarding sheep races, dandling our babies on my knee. If you enjoy finances, it's my duty to see that you may have as much diversion in that regard as you please—and as little burden. A duke knows all about duty, my dear, but he needs the right duchess to teach him about happily ever afters and true love."

* * * * *

A duck quacked somewhere out on the lake, and a breeze presumed to tease at Sedgemere's hair. His tone was very stern, but his eyes were no longer an arctic wilderness to Anne. His eyes held promises, and challenges, and such a steady regard her heart warmed to behold him.

That he'd puzzled out her situation didn't surprise her that much, though he'd found her out much more quickly than she'd anticipated. She had not, however, expected that his reaction would be to… solve her dilemma.

"I like money," she said, lest he mistake the matter. "I like making money grow like that magical beanstalk, and grow with the slow inexorability of the moonrise, grow every which way in between." Grow like her feelings for Sedgemere. "I like interest calculations, and formulas, and ledgers that balance to the penny. I can chase a missing penny for hours."

Sedgemere stood very close. "I can make love with you for hours."

Anne had enjoyed a taste of that, when she'd nearly torn his clothes from his body, and he'd met her frantic overtures with slow, steady, relentless desire. Sedgemere's self-control had taken her breath away, and driven her nearly to Bedlam at the thought of having to give him up.

She smoothed her fingers over the lock of his hair sent amiss by the wind. "I like money, I do not like being its slave, Sedgemere. You must keep your hand in the finances, help me manage Papa, and ensure I have time to hunt for lucky clovers."

She longed, not only to be rescued from her inherited burdens, but also to have all the happiness life as Sedgemere's wife and mother of his children could dream of. Wealth mattered not at all without somebody to share it.

Anne had learned that lesson four hundred thousand pounds ago. She had never learned how to beg, though. Sedgemere held her heart in his hands, and all she could do was await his decision.

He gazed out over the lake, his expression inscrutable. "Will you search for those treasures in the locations of my choosing? The lucky clovers and such? A few might be stashed in the places you've yet to thoroughly inspect."

Relief and gratitude, sweet and profound, coursed through Anne. She need not be her papa's abacus ever again—Sedgemere would intercede when she felt overburdened—and she need never carry another burden in solitary misery either.

"You are all the treasure I will ever need, Elias. You and the boys, and Joseph too, of course."

Sedgemere's arms came around her, Anne leaned into him, and before they returned to the house, she did, indeed, find an entire bouquet of lucky clovers in some very unlikely places.

EPILOGUE

"Anne looks different to me," Hardcastle said as he and Sedgemere sat down to the obligatory rare beefsteak and undercooked potato featured in London's most exclusive gentlemen's clubs. On a blustery late autumn day, the place at least had a roaring fire in its dining room. "She seems... happier."

Though how taking Sedgemere in hand could add to a woman's happiness, Hardcastle did not know. Sedgemere seemed happier too. He swore less frequently, reduced fewer presuming earls to quivering wrecks in the Lords, and no longer plagued Hardcastle night and day about finding a bride.

Tedious business, bride hunting, but Hardcastle's own grandmama had taken up the cudgels, and seeing Sedgemere and his duchess billing and cooing restored a man's faith in miracles. Thank goodness, Hardcastle had a nephew in the nursery to prevent Grandmama from declaring outright war on his bachelorhood. Finding the right duchess would require care and planning, nerves of steel, and a well-developed sense of martyrdom.

"Please pass the damned salt," Sedgemere snapped. "Are you quite well, Hardcastle? I'm not in the habit of repeating my requests."

"Yes, you are," Hardcastle replied, passing the salt cellar. "Until you get exactly what you want. When is the blessed event?"

The delicate silver spoon Sedgemere had been dredging through the salt paused. "Did Anne tell you?"

Well, damn. "You told me. Your step is lighter, you bring up the boys more often than you mention whatever scheme you're hatching with Moreland regarding the Corn Laws. You dragged me to a shop that sells kites last Tuesday. Marriage agrees with you. Ergo, a blessed event becomes likely."

Sedgemere sprinkled salt just so over his beefsteak. The potatoes were hopeless, but Hardcastle passed the butter anyway.

"I should become a papa again in the spring," Sedgemere said. "I'm shamelessly hoping for a daughter, and so are the boys. Don't think you're safe though."

Sedgemere was safe at last. A man at risk of becoming a stodgy old duke had been rescued by a banker's daughter and a few weeks of duck hunting, as it were. Hardcastle congratulated himself on having played matchmaker with no one the wiser.

"I am a duke," Hardcastle said, taking a sip of a red wine more hearty than delicate. "No one would dare harm my person. Ergo, I am safe. Grandmama would kill the matchmakers for even trying to usurp her right to plague me herself on the matter of matrimony."

"As would I, as would Anne, and the boys too. You are not safe, however, from the Duchess of Sedgemere's latest ambition. Aren't you having anything to eat?"

Ambitious duchesses ought to be outlawed by royal decree. Hardcastle poured himself more wine.

"I'd rather hear about these ambitions you've allowed your wife to develop, for I sense they do not bode well for your oldest and dearest friend." Also, possibly Sedgemere's loneliest friend, though a duke became inured to loneliness.

"Anne has your happiness in mind," Sedgemere said. "I'm mentioning her plans because you're owed a warning. Once the baby arrives, Anne will turn her attention to organizing a house party. She's been in correspondence with Her Grace of Veramoor, and your days as a single duke are numbered, my friend."

"This is the thanks I get for finding you a wife?" Hardcastle retorted. "For presiding at a duck orgy, and becoming godfather to no less than five waddling little god-ducklings? Now your own duchess is plotting a house party, and my name is on the guest list? Sedgemere, you disappoint me."

Though the betrayal was sweet. Sedgemere's duchess had him firmly in hand. Probably regularly in hand, too. Envy tried to crowd its way onto Hardcastle's dinner menu, but he fended it off by focusing on the threat immediately before him.

"When is this bacchanal to take place?" Hardcastle asked.

"You have plenty of time, not until summer, when all the best bacchanals take place. You might consider spending the summer in France."

Not again. France, Ireland, Scotland… Weariness joined envy as additions to the meal's offerings.

"Grandmama will never allow me to decline an invitation from Sedgemere House," Hardcastle said. "I suppose we'll have sheep races at this gathering too?"

Sedgemere sat back, crossing his knife and fork over his mostly empty plate. Marriage must give the man an appetite, for Hardcastle had found the food utterly ignorable.

"You're just jealous," Sedgemere said, which was true enough. "I'm the better sheep-race steward, and you know it. We probably will have sheep races too, because the boys are insistent that Christopher come along with you to the house party."

Christopher, the nephew who grew three inches every time Hardcastle visited the nursery.

"What do we have to do to get some trifle in this establishment?" Hardcastle muttered. "You'd have me drag an innocent child the length of the realm so he might be inducted into the royal order of sheep jockeys. My upbringing was deprived, I see that now."

His upbringing *had* been deprived, of course, so had Sedgemere's. They'd been ducal heirs from too young an age, not allowed to be boys much less rascals or sheep jockeys. Christopher deserved better, though hauling him from Kent up to Nottinghamshire would also mean...

"Hardcastle, that expression does not bode well for the king's peace."

"The poor king sired fifteen children," Hardcastle replied, signaling the waiter. "He'll never have peace again. If Christopher is to attend this house party—assuming it ever takes place—his governess will have to travel north with us and join the assemblage for the duration."

"Ah, the trifle arrives," Sedgemere said, as one waiter removed the dinner plates, and another set a frothy, fruity confection before each duke. "Eat up, Hardcastle. For nothing you can say or do, promise or threaten, will tempt me to get your name off Anne's guest list."

"Don't be needlessly puerile," Hardcastle said, taking a spoonful of creamy, delectable heaven. "I know my duty. Eat your trifle, Sedgemere. If Christopher and I are invited to this house party, to this house party we will go."

Though they would not go without Christopher's devoted governess, of that, Hardcastle was most certain.

THE END

To my dear Readers,

I hope you enjoyed Elias and Anne's story, and appreciate that I did not name it Duck of My Dreams. (I was tempted, but Hardcastle would have none of that.) His story is found in the anthology, ***Dancing in the Duke's Arms***, and is titled *May I Have This Duke?*

If you're in the mood for more ducal disporting, I recently joined Emily Greenwood and Susanna Ives in publishing the Regency novella anthology, ***Dukes in Disguise***. Three young, handsome dukes take to the shires to dodge the matchmakers, and run straight into the arms of true love. Funny how that always seems to happen.

My next full length Regency romance—**Jack—The Jaded Gentlemen, Book IV**—comes out in June 2016. I'm looking very much forward to Jack's tale, and have included an excerpt for you below.

If you'd like to be kept informed regarding all of my new releases, special offers, and events, you can sign up for my newsletter at GraceBurrowes.com/contact.php. I issue a newsletter several times a year, and will never sell or give away your address.

You can also find me on Facebook at Facebook.com/Grace-Burrowes-115039058572197/ and Twitter at Twitter.com/GraceBurrowes, or stop by the website at GraceBurrowes.com to browse the shelves and catch up on the news.

Read on for the opening scene from *Jack—The Jaded Gentlemen, Book IV!*

Grace Burrowes

Jack
The Jaded Gentlemen, Book IV

CHAPTER 1

"My poor, wee Charles is all but done for," Mortimer Cotton ranted. "This is the next thing to murder."

All poor, wee, wooly, twelve-stone of Charles—a ram of indiscriminate breed—lay flat out in the December sunshine as if dead from a surfeit of sexual exertions.

"Thievery has been committed under our very noses, Sir Jack," Cotton went on, meaty fists propped on his hips. "That woman stole my tup, bold as brass. Now look at him."

Charles II, as the ram was styled, would recover from his erotic excesses by sundown, if he ran true to his owner's boasts. Based on the contentment radiating from Hattie Hennessey's ewes, Charles had shared his legendary favors with the entire lot of them.

"Mark my words, Sir Jack: Slander is what we have here," Hattie retorted. "Mr. Cotton accuses me of stealing yon lazy tup, when he ought to be fined for not keeping his livestock properly contained. Now here the ram is, helping himself to my fodder, and to my poor yowes."

Cotton's complexion went from florid to choleric. "Your runty damned yowes haven't been covered by a proper stud since they were born, Hattie Hennessey. Do I hear gratitude for their good fortune? Do I hear a word about compensating me for poor Charles's generosity? No, I hear you blathering on about fines and insults to my integrity as a proper yeoman."

Opinion in the shire was usually divided regarding which injured party— for Hattie and Mortimer were perpetually offending each other—had the true grievance. In this case, Hattie had notified Sir Jack that a stray ram was loose among her ewes.

The very same ram Mortimer would have charged her a fortune to borrow for stud services.

"Mr. Cotton, might I have a word between us gentlemen—us human gentlemen?" Sir Jack interjected into the escalating insults.

"I'll give ye as many words as ye like. None of 'em fit for Charles's delicate ears."

While Cotton cast a baleful glance at his exhausted ram, Sir Jack winked at Hattie. She turned her regard on her ewes, the major source of her cash income, and very likely her dearest companions besides her collie and her cat.

Jack paced over to the far side of a hay rick, and Cotton followed a few fuming moments later.

"Hattie Hennessey has not the strength to wrestle your ram over stone walls," Sir Jack said, "much less carry him the distance from your farm to hers." This was not entirely true. Hattie Hennessey had the Hennessey family height and substance, even in old age. When in a temper she could likely subdue even a fractious ram.

She could not, however, ask for help from anybody under any circumstances, the Hennesseys being notoriously stubborn and independent—much like the Cottons.

"Then she hired this thievery done," Cotton shot back.

"I don't think so," Sir Jack replied, brushing a wisp of hay from his sleeve. "In the first place, she hasn't a single coin to spare. In the second, I think a certain neighbor, who is too kind for his own good, set the ram down among Hattie's ewes in the dark of night, thus saving a poor widow from begging for aid she desperately needs."

Cotton's bushy white brows beetled into a single line of consternation. "Mr. Belmont, maybe? Or his boys? Boys at that age would consider this a lark. Charles is the friendly sort, when he's not on the job."

Charles was an ovine hedonist. "I'm not accusing the Belmonts of wayward charity, Mr. Cotton. I'm accusing you."

Those brows shot up, and before Cotton could get out a word, Jack continued his theorizing. He'd learned serving in India that if senior officers were spared having to comment on a report prematurely, matters generally came to a more sensible conclusion.

"You know Hattie's circumstances would deteriorate if she couldn't replace the ram who died over the summer. You know she can't afford to go a year without a crop of lambs. Rather than affront her dignity with outright charity, you—or somebody with a charitable heart—concocted this scheme to spare her pride and put her situation to rights. I must say, I'm impressed. Vicar will likely be impressed as well."

Vicar had become so weary of the feud between Mortimer Cotton and

Hattie Hennessey that he'd taken to preaching successive sermons on the Good Samaritan.

Cotton's backside graced the church pews regularly. His coin was less frequently seen in the poor box.

"You think I *arranged* this, Sir Jack?"

Well, no, Jack thought no such thing, but needs must when the magistrate was at his wit's end. "Such a scheme has your stamp, Cotton, your sense of practicality and dispatch. But if we remain here much longer, congratulating you on your Christian virtues, Hattie will get out her pitchfork and chase that ram from the premises."

"She'll not abuse my Charles when he's spent from his labors. I'll not have it. Charles can't know which ewe belongs to which farm."

To Charles, every ewe belonged to him alone, for the span of a few minutes. Jack had known many an officer in His Majesty's army who'd taken a similar view of amatory pursuits.

"I can probably talk Hattie into allowing Charles to recover here for a day or two," Jack said, "until you can retrieve him. I wouldn't want anybody to say that such a fine animal was overtaxed by such a small herd." And in those two days, Charles would finish the job he'd started—likely finish it several times over.

"My Charlie, *overtaxed?*"

"We're agreed then. If I can talk Hattie around, Charles will rest from his labors, say until Thursday, at which point, I'll get him home to you. If you leave now in a fit of indignation, Hattie will be none the wiser regarding your generosity."

Cotton peered at Jack as if the word *generosity* was among the French phrases tossed about the Quality at fancy dress balls. To Mortimer Cotton, generosity was likely another word for foolishness, but he had as much pride as the next man. Jack could almost hear Cotton quoting Vicar's pious admonitions at the next darts tournament.

"You've found me out, Sir Jack," Cotton said, kicking at the dirt. "You'll not breathe a word to anybody? Hattie Hennessey is prouder than any Christian ought to be."

Oh, right. "You may rely on my discretion, Cotton. The plight of poor widows should concern more people in this shire, and I commend you for taking note of that."

"My sentiments exactly. I'll be on my way now, and trust to your, erm, discretion." Cotton bowed smartly and marched off across the barnyard, sparing Hattie the barest tip of his hat.

Hattie watched him go, her faded blue gaze considering. "It's well you sent that bag of wind from my property, Sir Jack, but he forgot to take his rutting tup with him."

"Rutting is what tups do, Hattie." What Jack hadn't done for far too long, come to that.

One of the ewes wandered over to sniff at Charles's recumbent form. Charles rallied enough to touch noses with his caller, then lay back in the straw with a great, masculine sigh. The ewe curled down next to him and began chewing her cud.

"Eloise," Hattie said, shaking a finger at the ewe, "you are a strumpet. Come spring, I'll expect twins from you, my girl."

Charles was known for siring twins and even the occasional batch of triplets.

"Hattie, I must impose on your good nature," Jack said, "for my dog cart won't be available to transport Charles home until Thursday. I went so far as to assure Cotton you'd not charge him board for the ram, nor bring a complaint for failure to properly contain his stock."

Hattie twitched another piece of straw from Jack's sleeve. "Getting airs above your station, Sir Jack, speaking on my behalf to that buffoon."

Jack was heir to a bachelor earl. His station was well above settling barnyard squabbles, but he'd rather have this discussion here than endure successive visits from Cotton and Hattie at Teak House.

"Cotton cannot have it bruited about that his stock is getting loose, Hattie. Show a little pity for a man who likely knows no peace before his own hearth."

Hattie's snort startled the resting ram. "That Perpetua Cotton has a lot of nerve, whining about this, sniffing about that, flouncing hither and yon with a new bonnet every week. Mortimer Cotton needs to take that woman in hand."

How exactly did a prudent man take in hand a grown woman with a wealth of thoroughly articulated opinions and ten children to keep clothed and fed?

"Mortimer Cotton is clearly a man overwhelmed," Jack said, holding a gloved hand out to a curious ewe. "Show him a bit of charity. Let the ram bide among your ewes until I can take him home later in the week."

The ewe sniffed delicately, then went about her business. Animals were, in so many ways, better behaved than people.

"Go on wi' ye," Hattie snapped, waving her hand at the ewe. The ewe trotted off a few steps, then took the place on Charles's other side. Sheep were naturally protective of one another, unlike people, apparently.

"I'd take it as a personal favor if you'd allow Charles to stay for a few days, Hattie."

Everything in Jack longed to grab a pitchfork and fill up the hayrick, then top up the water trough, and pound a nail through the loose board somebody had tied up to the fence post abutting the gate. Hattie would never allow him to set foot on the property again if he presumed to that extent.

"The ram can bide here," Hattie said, marching off toward the gate. "Until Thursday morning, no later."

"My thanks," Jack murmured, following. He opened the gate for her, and the creaking hinge woke his horse up. That fine fellow had been dozing at the hitching post outside Hattie's tiny cottage.

"You'll stay for a cup o' tea," Hattie announced. "Least I can do when you came straight away to deal with that plague against the commonweal."

Did Hattie refer to Mortimer or Charles?

"Perhaps another time, Hattie. I'm expected at Candlewick and have tarried too long as it is. Shall I bring over some hay for Mortimer's ram?"

Hattie stopped short, fists on hips, the same pose Cotton had adopted. "I'll not be taking charity, Sir Jack, if it's all the same to you. Mortimer Cotton has been farming this shire, boy and man, and if he doesn't realize his ram will eat my hay, then don't you be telling him. I'll have a crop of lambs, thanks to Mortimer's incompetence, though they'll likely be contrary and puny."

"I meant no insult," Jack said, taking up his gelding's girth. "I do apologize." He mentally apologized as well for declining her proffered cup of tea. Hattie was doubtless lonely, but Jack had already hit his limit of gratuitous socializing, and his day wasn't over.

"Apology accepted, this time," Hattie retorted, stroking a hand over the horse's nose. "If you see my little Maddie at Candlewick, tell her to pay a call on her old auntie, you hear?"

On Jack's most daring day, he'd hesitate to issue an order to Madeline Hennessey, who had not been little for many a year.

"I'll tell Miss Hennessey that you miss her."

He swung up on his horse and trotted out of the stable yard, while Charles, apparently recovered, climbed aboard the wayward Eloise and did what rams did best. Jack envied the sheep both his calling and the apparently boundless enthusiasm with which he so diligently pursued it.

Made in the USA
Lexington, KY
12 April 2016